"That's him! That's the man!"

The Executioner reacted swiftly, whipping the .38 from beneath his Windbreaker and triggering a shot. Then he was out the door and running for his life, his only chance for survival in reaching the barracks.

A salvo of slugs whizzed through the air, one striking at Bolan's abdomen, hitting a clip that was jammed into the warrior's belt. A cartridge in the mag detonated, the force of the blow knocking the Executioner off his feet, making him gasp in pain.

The warrior crawled the last few feet to the barracks door, used his subgun to force it open and rolled inside. He pulled the damaged magazine from his belt, tossed it aside, then pointed his weapon at the door. The soldiers had ceased firing, but they wouldn't hold back for long.

Bolan groaned as he climbed slowly to his feet and latched the door. He released the spent clip and rammed home the last full one. From now on every round had to count.

MACK BOLAN®

The Executioner

DON PENDLETON'S®

THE EXECUTIONER®

FEATURING MACK BOLAN®

EVIL CODE

A GOLD EAGLE BOOK FROM
WORLDWIDE®

TORONTO • NEW YORK • LONDON
AMSTERDAM • PARIS • SYDNEY • HAMBURG
STOCKHOLM • ATHENS • TOKYO • MILAN
MADRID • WARSAW • BUDAPEST • AUCKLAND

First edition September 1993

ISBN 0-373-61177-3

Special thanks and acknowledgment to
William Fieldhouse for his contribution to this work.

EVIL CODE

Do not seek evil gains; evil gains are the equivalent of disaster.

—Hesiod
700 B.C.

When ruthless greed and brutal ambition combine, the result is often a great evil. It is mandatory to root out that evil before all of humanity is threatened.

—Mack Bolan

THE
MACK BOLAN®
LEGEND

Nothing less than a war could have fashioned the destiny of the man called Mack Bolan. Bolan earned the Executioner title in the jungle hell of Vietnam.

But this soldier also wore another name—Sergeant Mercy. He was so tagged because of the compassion he showed to wounded comrades-in-arms and Vietnamese civilians.

Mack Bolan's second tour of duty ended prematurely when he was given emergency leave to return home and bury his family, victims of the Mob. Then he declared a one-man war against the Mafia.

He confronted the Families head-on from coast to coast, and soon a hope of victory began to appear. But Bolan had broken society's every rule. That same society started gunning for this elusive warrior—to no avail.

So Bolan was offered amnesty to work within the system against terrorism. This time, as an employee of Uncle Sam, Bolan became Colonel John Phoenix. With a command center at Stony Man Farm in Virginia, he and his new allies—Able Team and Phoenix Force—waged relentless war on a new adversary: the KGB.

But when his one true love, April Rose, died at the hands of the Soviet terror machine, Bolan severed all ties with Establishment authority.

Now, after a lengthy lone-wolf struggle and much soul-searching, the Executioner has agreed to enter an "arm's-length" alliance with his government once more, reserving the right to pursue personal missions in his Everlasting War.

1

It was supposed to be an easy job with a minimum of risk. So much for that notion, Mack Bolan thought, as he watched the two young men in the alley by the Golden Lotus restaurant. Neon light reflected along the shaved head of one of the youths, and the polished brass jewelry worn by the other sparkled with each motion of his head. They would have been less obvious if they carried flashlights.

Two more fledgling thugs approached the front of the restaurant, dressed in the style of so-called punk rock devotees. One guy wore black leather from head to toe with decorative chains dangling from his clothes like steel moss. His companion was clad in a long raincoat and sported a Mohawk haircut, dyed purple with yellow at the spikelike tips.

Mohawk opened his coat to grip a cutdown shotgun with both hands. Leather Boy pulled a stainless-steel revolver from his jacket. Bolan was sure the two in the alley were also packing iron.

The Executioner didn't know why these guys were about to hit the restaurant. Maybe they knew who was inside, or maybe they just picked tonight to rob the Golden Lotus. Whatever the reason, they presented Bolan with one hell of a problem, and he couldn't remain a spectator when the shooting started. Most of the people in the restaurant were innocent bystanders. They were about to find themselves in the middle of a firefight between combatants who didn't give a damn how much innocent blood was spilled in the battle.

This night's work had started out as simple surveillance and reconnaissance. Heroin was flooding into the United States at an incredible rate. Just the previous month the Feds had seized more than eighty kilos of heroin in San Francisco. Yet, the dope was still coming into the country with no sign of slowing down. Recently the majority of shipments appeared to be arriving on the East Coast.

Evidence suggested a Chinese Triad operation in New York City was involved with the delivery and marketing of the biggest shipments of H. This didn't surprise the Executioner. He was well aware of the Triad's activities from firsthand experience. He also knew that most police agencies were ineffective when dealing with the Triads.

One reason was that too many police departments still didn't consider the Triad a serious criminal organization. Although Interpol had circulated warnings to police throughout the world concerning Triads, many cops thought of Chinese criminals as small, disorganized gangs, small potatoes compared to the Mafia or the Medellín cartel. In reality the Triads were larger and better organized than either the Mob or the cocaine cartels.

Stony Man Farm had learned that a man named Jason Kwoon was connected with the New York heroin trade. A third-generation Chinese-American, Kwoon was known to be a member of the Hwang Shui Triad. He had recently opened a Swiss bank account and was making large cash deposits. He was being pretty slick and covert, but he wasn't good enough to slip past the computer hunting tactics of Stony Man's Aaron Kurtzman.

Bolan had spent the past several hours following Kwoon all over the Big Apple. It was a tiresome and monotonous task that seemed to be going nowhere.

Until Kwoon met a man at the parking lot by the United Nations Building and got into the stranger's black sedan. Bolan followed them from the UN along Franklin D. Roosevelt Drive, near the less-than-picturesque view of the East River. The sedan moved onto East 14th and turned onto Bowery, with the Executioner tailing at a discreet distance.

The pursuit led to Chinatown. Perhaps the most colorful district in New York City, the cultural change was dramatic after passing through East Village and Little Italy. Curio shops, markets and taverns were shoved together as if trying to cover every centimeter of space. Signs in English were accompanied by Chinese versions in bright red ideograms. Bolan continued to follow the sedan through the winding streets and masses of pedestrians until the car finally arrived at the Golden Lotus on Mott Street.

Five men were waiting for Kwoon and his companion at the restaurant. They were young, tough Asians, and the warrior had no doubts they were

Triad street soldiers. Probably a Hwang Shui sub-boss and four bodyguards. They went into the restaurant to discuss business over dinner.

The Executioner switched on a laser mike and fixed the beam on a window. Sound vibrations on the glass traveled back to the "Wonder Wagon"—a specially outfitted van that was his method of travel during the surveillance—on the laser to the receiver unit. A dozen conversations were recorded from the restaurant, which was no problem. Voiceprints could identify Kwoon and whoever answered him during conversation. The tapes would have to be analyzed, voices isolated and possibly translated into English, but that could be done at the Farm.

Bolan figured he had something important on Kwoon and the heroin connection. All he had to do was stay put and let the high-tech surveillance gear do the rest. Then he spotted the four punk hoods and knew the soft probe would suddenly turn hard.

THE WARRIOR WAS ALWAYS prepared for trouble. In addition to the Beretta 93-R in shoulder leather, Bolan had an arsenal of weapons in the wagon—assault rifles, subguns, explosives, even a mortar. He needed something for close quarters, yet with a controlled rate of fire to reduce risk to noncombatants.

The Executioner chose a time-honored favorite and grabbed an Uzi submachine gun. With a 32-round staggered box magazine, the Uzi could dissolve a lot of problems without reloading. The weapon weighed about four kilos, and the cyclic rate was roughly 650 rounds per minute. The machine pistol was excellent for controlled fire, and the sights were suitable for accurate fire up to 100 yards. Bolan would be closer than that. A lot closer.

He shoved several spare magazines into his jacket pockets and slapped back the cocking knob at the top of the receiver. Bolan chambered the first round, set the selector switch to single shot and emerged from the van. The four punks had already entered the restaurant, and the first shots were fired before the Executioner could cross the street.

He reached the front door and entered low, the Uzi up and ready. As he feared, the punk invaders had immediately triggered a violent reaction from the Triad hit men. The Chinese gangsters had knocked over tables and found cover by the pillar supports as they exchanged fire with the would-be robbers. Restaurant customers and employees screamed and darted about in frenzied panic. Some had enough sense to hit the floor or seek shelter from the bullets and buckshot that sizzled through the dining room.

The punks had thought their strategy was pretty clever. Two through the front and two through the kitchen seemed to be a way to catch everybody off guard and stuck between potential cross fire. Unfortunately for them the Triad had expected a backup team from the kitchen the moment the first pair of youths appeared at the front entrance.

The two gunners who attacked from the kitchen were cut down before they could fire a shot. One of them held a cook for a human shield, but the Triad hardman couldn't have cared less, blasting the hostage along with the gunmen. The three bodies were sprawled by the kitchen entrance, a crimson puddle staining the floor beneath them.

Mohawk and Leather Boy managed a little better than their pals, taking cover behind a buffet table when the Triad gunners went into action. Leather Boy had stopped a bullet with his chest, but the slug had struck high enough to miss his heart or lungs. The punks had apparently used a chemical stimulus to charge up their courage for the robbery, which also reduced their pain level. Leather Boy thought he was Superman, unaware that he was bleeding to death.

A Triad gunman behind an overturned table fired an Ingram MAC-10 at the remaining punks. The spray of 9 mm slugs ripped across the room, smashing bottles and glasses behind a bar near his enemies but completely missing his intended targets.

Bolan dived behind a large brass gong next to the cash register. He raised the Uzi and fired two shots, both rounds drilling the gunner with the Ingram in the the face.

Enemy fire raked the Executioner's position, and he hugged the floor as slugs hammered the gong and shattered glass from the cabinet displays by the register. Mohawk shouted a curse and fired his shotgun. Buckshot tore a chunk from a tabletop, but a Chinese pistol man returned fire and hit Mohawk in the shoulder. The impact spun him, but the punk jacked the pump to his riot gun before he dropped behind cover.

Leather Boy left cover and triggered his revolver, a wide grin on his sweat-covered face. An Ingram responded, and he suddenly realized he wasn't Superman after all. His black jacket was riddled with bullet holes. One round sparked against one of his chains before it ricocheted upward to gouge a bloody tunnel in his left cheek.

Bolan adjusted the selector switch to full-auto as Mohawk blasted the Ingram gunner with a burst of 12-gauge fury. The buckshot smashed the head and shoulders of the Triad hit man, nearly decapitating him. Mohawk shouted a victory yell, as if avenging the death of Leather Boy somehow meant that he had won the conflict.

The last punk ducked in time to avoid a volley of pistol rounds. He pumped his shotgun and glimpsed motion in his peripheral vision. A boy, about ten years old, was running to his parents by the archway of a rest room. Mohawk laughed and pointed his gun at the child.

Bolan let loose a burst that blasted the riot gun from the punk's hands and punched him to the floor. Whatever drugs the guy had favored, his addiction was cured forever.

The Triad gunners could now focus on Bolan. They concentrated their firepower on the warrior's position, pinning him.

The Executioner thrust the stubby barrel of the Uzi between the base of the gong and the cabinet. He estimated the position of the Triad hardmen by the nearest table and opened fire.

High-velocity slugs splintered the tabletop, punching through the veneer to find the enemy. One man screamed and flopped to the floor, his body thrashing wildly in a convulsion of death. The second hit man rolled away from the table, wounded and disoriented. He didn't realize he had presented a clear target for his enemy.

Bolan drew his Beretta 93-R and triggered two shots. Both 9 mm projectiles struck the hardman in the chest, the 124-grain hollowpoints expanding when they hit, turning bone into splinters.

The surviving Triad gunner bolted for the kitchen while Bolan was busy with the two table defenders. He recognized Jason Kwoon and the well-dressed man from the UN. The third opponent brought up the rear and elected to stay by the doorway to fire at Bolan's position and buy the others a few seconds of time.

The Triad killer's .45 automatic roared twice. One round smashed into the cash register and sent a shower of coins across the floor. The other hit a plastic dragon on the wall and broke off one of its legs. Bolan returned fire with the Beretta. He aimed high and tore out a chunk of the door frame above the gunman's head. The Chinese hitter ducked and dropped to one knee.

Bolan opened fire with the Uzi in his other fist, a trio of parabellum rounds punching his opponent backward into the kitchen, dead. The warrior jumped to his feet and headed for the front door.

He stepped outside and saw a yellow Honda hastily pull away from a parking space next to the alley. Jason Kwoon and his well-dressed companion stared at the Executioner through the windshield.

The warrior aimed the Beretta, but the Honda turned sharply onto the street and he held his fire. The vehicle boldly cut in front of a Checker cab and nearly slammed into the rear of a beer truck. Kwoon came close to an accident, but he managed to avoid a collision and put more distance between the Honda and the Executioner.

Bolan was not willing to risk hitting civilians. Kwoon and his mysterious companion would have to wait. He heard the wail of police sirens grow closer and knew he had to get out of the area himself.

The Executioner jogged to the black sedan parked by the restaurant. Two flags were attached to antenna at the hood—one the familiar blue-and-white banner of the United Nations, the other red with a blue rectangle in the upper corner and an odd symbol in the middle, surrounded by a circle of small white stars. Bolan had seen the flag before, but wasn't certain what country it represented.

He glanced inside the sedan. The tinted glass didn't reveal much, but he suspected anything of interest would be in the trunk. The warrior moved to the rear of the car and blasted the lock on the trunk with a short burst from the Uzi. The latch gave and the trunk popped open.

Inside sat four suitcases. Bolan drew a combat knife from a boot sheath and used the blade to spring the locks to the first case. It opened to reveal more than a dozen clear plastic bags filled with white powder—about twenty kilos of heroin, the warrior guessed. If the rest of the baggage held as much dope, it would have been a hell of a big buy.

The Executioner left the heroin for the police and headed across the street. His van was hidden from view of the restaurant and pointed toward a side street. If he hurried, Bolan could be on Park Row in two or three minutes. Then he could cross the bridge into Brooklyn before police could finish questioning eyewitnesses at the Golden Lotus.

If he hurried . . .

2

A close-up of a photograph Bolan had taken during his surveillance of Jason Kwoon flashed onto the screen.

"Okay," Hal Brognola began. "What we have here is a diplomat's car and the flag of the country he represents—the Union of Myanmar. Until it changed its name in 1989, Myanmar was called Burma."

"Burma," Bolan repeated. "Part of the Golden Triangle."

"So we have a pretty clear idea where the heroin has been coming from," the big Fed stated.

"You have a positive ID on the guy?"

Brognola clicked the slide projector, and the well-dressed man who had met Kwoon at the United Nations appeared on the screen. Bolan got a better look at the guy's face. His features were more calm and pleasant than when he saw them the night before. The dark almond-shaped eyes seemed bright and shrewd. The upward corners of the mouth seemed confident in the photograph, perhaps even arrogant.

"This is Maung Gawbyan," Brognola said, as he checked his notes in an effort to pronounce the name correctly. "He's a member of the diplomatic corps of Myanmar. Part of a delegation at the United Nations."

"Don't tell me. He has diplomatic immunity, and the police and the federal government can't touch him."

"Right, unfortunately," Brognola replied. "Maung Gawbyan can't be legally arrested for attempting to sell heroin to the Hwang Shui Triad or smuggling it into the United States. Probably had the drugs shipped in to his office in one or more diplomatic pouches. Some of those things are pretty big."

"And we don't know how long Maung Gawbyan has been getting heroin into the U.S. using those pouches," Bolan said with a nod. "No way we can have them searched if more come in from Burma...I mean Myanmar?"

"Look, for simplicity's sake, let's refer to it as Burma. To answer your question, no way. That's part of diplomatic immunity. It's regarded as necessary for diplomats to be able to maintain complete security and be fully protected while doing government business in foreign countries. Of course, diplomatic immunity can be very positive. We wouldn't want American diplomats serving in a hostile country to be arrested by the secret police to be held hostage or tortured. We wouldn't want confidential papers concerning our relations with another country to be seized by anyone curious about our more covert dealings abroad."

"I know how it's supposed to work. I'm also well aware that Stony Man Farm has used contacts with our embassies to transport weapons and equipment in diplomatic pouches that would have been pretty tough to smuggle into another country when I've needed the hardware in the field.''

Brognola grinned. ''Well, I don't think that was the reason diplomatic immunity was established, but it has been useful for us in the past. Of course, it's been handy for intel outfits like the CIA. When our guys do it, we approve of immunity and diplomatic pouches that can't be searched by the authorities. When the other side does it, we're not so thrilled with the system.''

''You can't please all of the people all of the time,'' Aaron Kurtzman remarked as he rolled his wheelchair from the elevator.

The computer wizard continued to be an active member of the Stony Man team despite being confined to the chair. A bullet in the spine had left him partially paralyzed, but stronger than ever in spirit and determination. Kurtzman was a constant source of inspiration to Bolan. He still seemed big and burly even in the wheelchair. Kurtzman's nickname, the Bear, still suited him.

Kurtzman approached the conference table and handed some computer printout sheets and faxed photographs to Brognola.

''Here's the information available on the dudes who got wasted in the shootout last night. The police haven't been able to identify a couple of the Chinese gunmen. FBI doesn't have fingerprints on file that match those of the dead men. Names they were using were probably fake. Seems likely they were covertly imported from the Far East. The Hwang Shui outfit is international, and its home base is believed to be in Hong Kong."

"Anything else?" Brognola asked.

"One of the Chinese who was identified is believed to be a fairly big fish in the Triad pool. Sort of a subchief in charge of drug trafficking in New York City. Of course, information on anything about Hwang Shui operations is limited."

"Any of the dead men have previous criminal history?" Brognola asked. "Rap sheets have anything on assault, robbery, drug pushing? Maybe not heroin. Could be they started selling marijuana or cocaine."

"A couple of them had been arrested for stuff in the past, but charges were dropped. No connection with any drugs except heroin."

"The various Triads don't deal in any other type of narcotics," Bolan said. "They specialize in heroin and only that produced from the poppy fields in Asia."

"That's what my research shows too, Striker."

"What about the four weirdos who hit the restaurant?" Brognola asked. "Any way they knew the Triad was making a deal with the Burmese diplomat, or did they just plan to rob the place?"

"They're all dead, Hal," Kurtzman replied. "Who knows? They had criminal records and armed robbery seemed to be their expertise."

"I think they just picked the wrong night to rob the restaurant," Bolan said. "We had surveillance on

Kwoon. Never saw any sign of those four until last night.''

"How about Jason Kwoon?'' the big Fed asked. "We have enough to have him arrested. Maybe we can't touch Maung Gawbyan, but Kwoon doesn't have diplomatic immunity.''

"I don't know what's going to be done about him,'' Kurtzman admitted. "I doubt he'll be stupid enough to go home after what happened. He'll probably ditch the car he used last night and find shelter with the Triad.

"Gadgets is still going over the tape recordings with voice analysis equipment, translating machines and that sort of stuff,'' the Bear went on. "It'll take awhile, but we'll know exactly what they were discussing in the restaurant before the robbery occurred.''

"We don't have to wait to know what was coming down,'' Bolan told him. "It's obvious. Gawbyan brought the heroin from Myanmar and he was going to sell it to the New York Triad. That's what the drug trade is all about—money.''

Hal Brognola unwrapped a cigar and stuck it in his mouth. "Okay. An official complaint can be made to their embassy or the delegation at the UN. Gawbyan might have diplomatic immunity, but his government isn't going to be too happy with him using it to smuggle drugs and sell them to the Chinese Mob in the U.S.''

"What will they do with him?'' Kurtzman asked. "Send him back to Myanmar with a slap on the wrist?''

"They might do a lot more than slap his wrist," Brognola replied. "I've read over the recent reports of Myanmar's justice system. Amnesty International and other groups concerned with human-rights violations say that things are pretty bad there. Trials are less than fair, people are thrown into hellhole prisons, and torture is frequently used by the security forces. Lots of executions take place, too. Gawbyan might face a more strict punishment for his crimes when he goes home than he could face here."

"And maybe he won't," the Executioner said. "Gawbyan must have gotten his job as a diplomat because he has friends in high places. That means there's a good chance he'll be able to skate past any serious punishment. The people in authority seldom get judged by the same standards as the average Joe. That's true everywhere, but especially in a police state."

"Even growing opium poppies has been illegal in Burma for decades," the big Fed insisted. "I don't think they changed that when the country became Myanmar. Gawbyan could be in big trouble."

"You read the reports on human-rights violations," Bolan said. "What did Amnesty International and the others say was the reason most of those people stood trial? Were they accused of heroin trafficking or criticizing the state? Were the people tortured or put in prison members of the ruling-class elite, or poor and middle class who protested government policies? How many have been executed for making multimillion-dollar dope deals?"

Brognola nodded. The record of human-rights violations in Myanmar had been directed against protestors, not government officials. There was a good chance the warrior's suspicions that Gawbyan would go unpunished was accurate. The big Fed sighed.

"Look, Striker. You know we can't solve all the world's ills and stop injustice everywhere. You stopped ninety kilos of heroin from winding up on the street. That's pretty good. Sometimes you have to accept what victory you can get and try not to fret about things that are out of your control."

"I'm not convinced this is over," the Executioner said. "We don't know how much heroin Gawbyan might still have or whether he'll be able to arrange another sale with the Triad before he's sent back to Myanmar."

"And you intend to find out?" Brognola asked. "The Burmese delegation won't take kindly to anyone snooping around. If you trespass, the embassy personnel will be within their rights to regard it as a hostile invasion. That means they can shoot you on sight."

Bolan arched a brow. "Hal, I'm used to that."

3

The Burmese diplomats might have been attached to the United Nations, but their government had rented an estate in upstate New York. Working in Manhattan was one thing, living there was another. The Big Apple was too crowded, too noisy and too dangerous for anyone to live there if it could be avoided.

Because they were in a position to do so, the Burmese delegation had picked an expensive twenty-room mansion far from the crowds of Manhattan. It was surrounded by forest and an electrified gate. Monthly rent and utilities cost a not-so-small fortune. The officials from Myanmar had not been making payments for the past three months, but there were no plans to evict them or cut off power to the estate. Diplomatic immunity again, Bolan thought.

The Executioner observed the estate from the branches of a pine tree. The building was big, and surveillance cameras were posted outside the mansion, standard models that revolved in a set pattern to scan certain areas of the grounds. They were easier to avoid than most people realized.

Thanks to Stony Man's limitless sources of information, Bolan had seen blueprints of the building and knew details about the alarm system, fire fighting ceiling sprinklers and the type of wiring used to electrify the fence. These had all been installed since the delegation from Myanmar had moved in, and the modifications had been done by local companies that specialized in expensive home security. Information about the systems was on file, and Stony Man had access.

However, Bolan learned that some things hadn't been discovered by Kurtzman's computer taps. Two guards patrolled the estate grounds, accompanied by trained Doberman pinschers.

The Executioner had anticipated such security measures and prepared for them. He climbed down from the tree and landed silently on the rubber soles of his boots. Dressed in his black suit and with his face smeared with black combat cosmetics, the warrior blended with the darkness. By the base of the tree trunk lay a small black buttpack. He buckled it around his narrow waist as he went over a short mental inventory of his gear.

Bolan carried an unusual array of nonlethal weapons for the mission. A Bio-Inoculator was holstered on his hip. Used to tranquilize large animals, either in zoos or in the wild, the BI pistol was powered by a CO_2 cartridge. The butt magazine carried three darts, each loaded with 150 milligrams of Thorazine. A bulky, awkward device that resembled an oversize pellet pistol, it wasn't the sort of weapon the warrior ordinarily carried even for a soft probe. He didn't trust anything as unreliable as a tranquilizer dart that could vary drastically in effect on an individual's physical constitution.

The warrior didn't have great faith in the chemical Mace clipped to his shirt pocket or the Nova XR500 Stun Gun attached to his belt. The guards weren't the enemy. They were just doing their job, defending the diplomatic interests of their country. Bolan related to that. He knew about duty.

He checked the wind, the breeze stroking his face. At least he wasn't downwind as he approached the estate, but he knew the breeze could change at any moment and the keen senses of the dogs would detect him before he could enter the grounds. The soldier had to act quickly. He could avoid the cameras and possibly the human sentries, but he knew he couldn't slip past the ultrasensitive noses and ears of the watchdogs. A confrontation was inevitable.

Bolan stayed low and crept to the fence, stretching flat on the ground as the camera rotated toward his position. He waited for it to move before he opened the pack. Without the lens pointed in his direction, the warrior quickly removed a long insulated cord that had alligator clips attached to each end. He snapped one clip to the fence, teeth fitted to the wire that ran along the base of the fence, then attached the other clip to the barrier two yards from the first. This bypassed the electrical charge to the fence within the portion between the two clips.

He hid from the camera once more, waited for the scanning electronic eye to pass and took a wire cutter from his bag. Bolan cut through the neutralized portion of fence and snipped out an opening roughly one yard high and one yard across. The warrior avoided the camera again before slithering through the hole. He set the cutout section of the fence back against the barrier. It wouldn't be noticed unless someone was carefully looking for it.

The angry snarls and barking of the Dobermans announced that Bolan's entry hadn't gone unnoticed by the animals. Bolan sprinted to the mansion and reached the wall beneath the metal pole that supported the nearest surveillance camera. He jammed the blades of the wire cutter under the camera and stuck it into the disk beneath, which blocked the gears and froze the camera in place. Unable to rotate, the camera would be able to cover only a single section of the grounds.

There was no point in trying to hide from the dogs. Bolan moved behind a row of well-manicured shrubs and waited for the animals to arrive. The first Doberman appeared two seconds after the Executioner took cover. The powerful dog towed its handler as it raced toward the warrior's position. The guard was barely able to hold on to the leash with one hand, while the other was on a button-flap holster on his hip.

The Executioner aimed the Bio-Inoculator and squeezed the trigger. The CO_2 gas hissed as the dart jetted from the barrel. The guard gasped in pain and surprise when the projectile struck his chest and he released the leash to claw at the dart. The Thorazine took effect rapidly. He dropped to one knee as he fumbled with the flap to his holster. The guy almost managed to draw his side arm before he passed out on the ground.

The Doberman charged. A streak of black and brown shot at Bolan, its jaws open to display a mouthful of white dagger teeth. The warrior fired the BI pistol, then raised his arm to protect his throat from the lunging teeth. The animal's body and momentum forced the Executioner backward, the BI pistol jarred from his hand as he hit the ground. He drew his Ka-bar combat knife, ready to fight the Doberman at close quarters.

The dog lay on its side, a tranquilizer dart lodged in its neck. The animal seemed confused and groggy. It lifted its head and bared its teeth in a final act of defiance before it surrendered to the chemical sleep of the Thorazine. Bolan put the knife away and started to get to his feet. He glanced around for the BI pistol, saw it and prepared to reclaim the weapon.

The bushes seemed to explode as another blur of dark fur and flashing fangs attacked. Bolan dropped to a kneeling stance and yanked the Mace from his pocket. He sprayed the concentrated tear gas at the face of the second attack dog, who twisted in midair and landed in an awkward skid across the grass. Its head bobbed wildly and its snarls changed to whimpers. The highly developed sense of smell that was the dog's greatest advantage as a hunter also made it especially vulnerable to the chemical spray.

The second guard approached with care. He had released his dog to find the intruder and followed from a distance, pistol already in hand. The man was surprised and alarmed to discover the Doberman on the ground, rubbing its muzzle in the grass in a frenzied effort to clear its nostrils. He glanced at a pair of nearby sycamores, then turned his attention to the shrubbery. Something moved among the bushes. Gun in hand, the sentry moved closer.

He cursed in his native Burmese when he saw the other Doberman among the shrubs, the animal stirring in a fitful sleep. Probably drugged, the guard guessed as he reached for a two-way radio on his belt. Someone had breached their security, and he figured he had better report it to the watch commander.

Bolan stepped from behind a tree trunk, creeping closer to the unsuspecting guard and unclipping the Nova Stun Gun from his belt. As the man raised the radio and prepared to key a transmission, the Executioner's free hand slashed a hard chop to the guard's wrist above the pistol. The gun fell from the man's fingers as he cried out and started to turn.

The warrior jammed the twin prongs of the XR500 under the sentry's ribs and pressed the plastic trigger. Thirty-five thousand volts of nonlethal electricity shot through the guard's body. The jolt was massive, but the Nova didn't use amps so the charge could stun without killing. The man fell to all fours, trembling from the effect of the shock. Bolan drew his Beretta and rapped the hardman behind the ear to knock the guy unconscious.

The Executioner dragged the second guard to where the first lay. Both men had handcuffs on their belts and he proceeded to cuff them together. Then he picked up their guns, radios and handcuff keys and threw them into the shrubs out of sight. As Bolan bent to retrieve the Bio-Inoculator, the gun hissed. He frowned as he picked it up. The CO_2 cartridge had been ruptured when it fell.

So much for that, he thought as he discarded the BI. He'd have to finish the probe without the sleep darts. Experience had taught him that something usually went wrong during a mission. The Executioner hoped that was it.

THE WATCH COMMANDER realized something was wrong. He hadn't been unduly alarmed when one of the cameras froze in place. The equipment was always malfunctioning, and it wasn't uncommon for a camera to cease rotating. However, he saw the dogs behave in an alarmed manner when he looked at the other monitors. The Dobermans and the guards headed in the same direction to investigate, moving toward the dysfunctional camera.

Neither man had radioed in a report to announce a raccoon or an opossum had gotten into the estate, which had happened before and triggered an attack response from the dogs. This was clearly more serious. The watch commander couldn't even find the sentries on the monitors. He grabbed his gun belt and headed for the door. They had a problem. A real security problem. He turned the knob and opened the door.

A chemical spray filled his eyes and nose. His mouth opened, and more concentrated CN–CD gas entered his throat. Choking and blinded by the unexpected attack, the guard staggered back into the monitor room, hands clasped to his face. Bolan stepped forward and swung a karate chop to the side of the dazed man's neck. The commander dropped unconscious to the floor.

The Executioner closed the door. He used the guard's own cuffs to manacle him to a swivel chair. Bolan looked at the monitors as he removed the magazine from the commander's pistol and dropped the empty gun into a wastebasket. Everything looked quiet outside.

The intel acquired from Stony Man was paying off. Bolan easily disconnected the burglar alarm to the house before he picked the lock to a door. Thanks to the inside information about the surveillance setup, the warrior knew exactly where the monitor center for the close-circuit TV network was located.

He glanced at his wristwatch: 0217. Things were going more or less on schedule, but he hadn't put a rigid time limit on the operation.

Bolan retrieved the watch commander's cap and donned it as he left the room and walked into the corridor. The lights were dim, and he knew security guards were usually taken for granted and hardly noticed by people accustomed to their presence. He hoped no one would give him a second look if he was seen patrolling the mansion. The place was quiet. With a little luck, everybody would be asleep. He could be in and out in a matter of minutes.

The Executioner entered a spacious den. A lone figure sat on a leather sofa, watching a black-and-white movie on television. Several long-neck beer bottles were in an ice bucket on the coffee table and a number of empties were lined up next to it. The guy barely glanced over his shoulder as Bolan strolled past the sofa.

Bolan knew the top-ranking diplomats had offices in the house as well as at the UN. A lot of desks and filing cabinets had been delivered to the estate, and the delegation was known to bring fellow UN representatives to the place for more relaxed conversations. People tended to pick sleeping quarters upstairs and workplaces down. Bolan started looking on the first floor.

He soon found a row of walnut doors with name plates on the panels. Luckily the printing was in roman letters as well as Burmese script. Bolan read the name Maung Gawbyan on one door. The soldier opened a leather packet to remove two lock picks. He knelt by the door, inserted the picks in the keyhole and probed inside the lock. He felt the pin tumblers and carefully worked them until he turned the picks. A click inside the lock rewarded his efforts. Bolan turned the knob and opened the door.

The Executioner entered the office, closed the door and switched on a small penlight. Gawbyan had a nice setup. The furniture was leather and the desk was large, polished wood. Bolan crept along the dense carpet to the desk. He took several button microphones from his pack and peeled off the back covers to expose the glue-coated sides.

Designed to stick to virtually any flat surface, the button mikes were ideal for discreet electronic eavesdropping. Bolan placed two to the underside of the desk, another along the back of the bookcase, one at the base of a floor lamp and under a shelf.

He wished he had time to search the entire building for any diplomatic pouches Gawbyan might have stored there. Of course, it was possible the smuggler had hidden the heroin elsewhere. No plan was perfect. Bolan had to settle for what he could accomplish one step at a time. He moved to the door and used the lock picks to secure it once more.

Bolan headed for the den. The guy who had been watching the TV had finally drunk himself to sleep and snored loudly as he lay on the sofa. The Executioner crossed the room and moved to the corridor. Two figures suddenly appeared from an open door. Young, physically fit, dressed in T-shirts and sweatpants, the pair stared at Bolan. The warrior knew the dim light wouldn't be enough protection against discovery. The new arrivals saw a big Caucasian under the service cap and realized he didn't belong there.

The warrior's instincts and training made him reach for the Beretta holstered under his arm. He altered the draw and grabbed the can of Mace instead. The delay was a fragment of a second, but enough time for one of the guards to launch a well-aimed kick. A sneaker-shod foot sent the Mace can flying from Bolan's fingers. The second man swung a fist at the Executioner's face.

Bolan weaved away from the rocketing knuckles and dealt his opponent a solid left hook to the cheekbone. The guy staggered from the punch, but his companion suddenly slammed a kick to Bolan's ribs. The blow sent the warrior stumbling into the back of the second man. He thrust a karate side-kick to the abdomen of the first guy before the Burmese kickboxer could follow his attack with another series of blows.

The second man surprised Bolan and snapped his head upward to butt the back of his skull into the warrior's face. Pain flashed white light across his eyes, but Bolan yanked the Nova Stun Gun from his belt in response.

His opponent whirled and lashed a backfist at Bolan's head. The Executioner ducked the attack and thrust the stun gun beneath the man's extended arm. The prongs stabbed the guy's armpit, and Bolan hit him with 35,000 volts. The electrical shock lifted the man off his feet and pitched him to the floor, his body trembling in agony.

Bolan saw a foot lash out and pulled his head back to avoid the attack. The remaining opponent had thrown another high kick and missed the warrior's face by scant inches. The guy was quick and threw a left hook when the kick missed. Bolan blocked with his right forearm and slashed his left hand at his assailant's neck. The chop hit the man's collarbone, and it stunned the man. The Executioner quickly jammed the Nova into his opponent's solar plexus, and a jolt of nonlethal electricity took the guy out of play.

The Executioner glanced at the drunk asleep on the sofa. The man continued to snore in blissful ignorance of the violence that had occurred within three yards of him. Bolan headed through the corridor to the door. He stepped outside to find the two security guards on their feet. Still handcuffed together, groggy and dazed, the pair staggered forward on unsteady legs.

Bolan drew the Beretta. The pair raised their hands, handcuff chain rattling between their wrists. The warrior didn't say a word, but kept his eye on the guards as he walked to the fence. They stood in place, arms high, expressions of weary defeat on their faces. The sentries watched Bolan slip through the hole in the fence. At that moment they didn't feel ashamed, disappointed or concerned about the reaction of their superiors to their failure to protect the estate. They were just glad to see the man in black go.

4

The aroma of freshly brewed coffee greeted Mack Bolan as he awakened from a light sleep. He sat up on the cot and saw the familiar face of Gadgets Schwarz. A dull pain in his side made the warrior wince.

"Still got a headache?" Schwarz inquired.

"No, but I still feel like I have that sentry's shoe imprinted on my ribs."

"That's what happens when you fight with a couple of *bando* boxers," Schwarz said. "*Bando* is a kind of kick-boxing. Read about that in a reference book."

"Is that how you've been spending your time?" Bolan asked, rising from the cot and moving to the coffeepot. The back of the Wonder Wagon wasn't large, but it was outfitted with everything from a built-in kitchenette to sophisticated surveillance equipment. A radio transceiver unit was among the latter, and Schwarz sat beside it, the reels of a tape recorder turning slowly as the voices continued to speak from the radio.

As his name suggested, Gadgets was an electronic wizard. Slender, with graying hair, he was a veteran commando who had fought many battles in Vietnam, on the streets and with Stony Man's Able Team. He had fought some battles alongside the Executioner, and Bolan figured Schwarz was a good man for any situation and possibly the best for surveillance.

"Well, there hasn't been much for me to do, Mack," Schwarz said. "I don't understand Burmese, so all I can do is sit here while the conversation comes in and tape it to be translated later."

Bolan sipped some coffee. "Is that coming from the bugs I planted or a laser mike?"

"The bugs."

"How long have they been talking?"

"More than half an hour," Schwarz replied. "They don't sound too happy, but it's kind of hard to tell. Voice inflections are different in Burmese than in English or other European languages. It's a Sino-Tibetan language, and different voice tones can completely change the meaning of a word. Same as with Chinese. However, Burmese writing is based on Sanskrit, not ideograms."

"How many reference books did you read?"

"You can never learn too much." Schwarz grinned.

A knock at the rear door of the van drew their attention. Schwarz reached for his .357 Magnum. Bolan waved at him to keep the gun in the holster. He had a pretty good idea who was outside.

"You guys awake in there?" a voice inquired.

Bolan opened the door, and Leo Turrin entered. The little Fed handed the Executioner a paper bag filled with pastries, claiming that they were some of the best cheese Danish in Manhattan.

"The delegation from Myanmar is raising hell," Turrin said. "They're complaining to the local and state police, FBI, Justice and just about everybody else. They're real pissed that somebody broke into their property last night. Well, I guess technically it happened early this morning."

Turrin poured himself a cup of coffee and fished a Danish from the bag as he continued. "Anyway, the diplomatic team is saying the U.S. is full of criminals and our police can't control them. No shit, huh? So, everybody is investigating the case. Justice Department put me in charge of our liaison with the Burmese diplomats."

The little Fed was a member of the Stony Man team, but he usually operated through the Justice Department.

"Guess Justice has to assign *somebody* to keep the diplomats happy," Schwarz observed.

"What did the delegates say about the break-in?" Bolan asked. "Do they suspect it's linked to Gawbyan's heroin trafficking?"

"They're still pretending that isn't true," Turrin replied. "If they do suspect a connection, they're not talking about it. The most popular theory seems to be the SAD is responsible."

"What the hell is the SAD?" Gadgets asked.

"The Social Affairs Department," Turrin answered. "Sounds like an outfit that arranges picnics and square dances, but it's really the sort of quaint name of the primary intelligence network of Mainland China. Burma may have changed its name, but the officials of Myanmar are still paranoid about China.''

"So nobody described the person who broke into the estate?"

"I didn't hear anybody make descriptions. They referred to the 'invaders,' so I guess they figure more than one guy was involved. They did mention Mace and sleep darts were used on the sentries and guard dogs."

"What's the status on Gawbyan? I take it charges have been made about him selling narcotics in Chinatown. The heroin was in the trunk of his car. The delegation can't ignore that, and he'd have a tough time explaining how it got there."

"He claims it was planted in his car," Turrin replied.

"God..." Schwarz said. "And they believe him?"

"I'm not sure if they do or not, but Gawbyan has an alibi. Sort of. He claims he was with two of his aides. They parked the sedan by the Golden Lotus and went for a walk in Chinatown. He says he was about a block from the restaurant when the shooting started. They realized it would be dangerous to go back to the car, but they were afraid to hang around the neighborhood. So, Gawbyan says, they got a taxi and headed back to the delegation at the UN."

"Did you ask him which cab company they used?"

"Said it was a gypsy cab. You know those free-lance drivers are all over the Big Apple. Anyway, the aides back up his bullshit story and claim they were with him."

"They're going to let him stay in the country?" Bolan asked.

"They plan to send him back to Myanmar until this...I think they called it an 'unpleasantness' blows over. Which means he might be back in a year. Maybe less. Not the way we wanted things to turn out, but I'm afraid that's it, Striker."

"Maybe not. I'm not convinced this is over. Let's see what we get from the tapes before we pack it in."

THE WONDER WAGON was parked at a clearing in the forest about half a mile from the Burmese estate. The van didn't attract any special attention because it stood on a camping site. They had even set up a hammock between two trees and placed a couple of lawn chairs outside.

The site was ideal for Bolan and Schwarz to conduct surveillance on the estate. They were within effective range for clear radio reception from the button microphones and laser mike scans. The phone lines to the estate had also been tapped at a trunk box about one mile from the property. The phones at the United Nations had also been tapped, just in case.

Bolan didn't think the UN phones would produce anything useful. Gawbyan would have been a total idiot to discuss illegal business on the telephone, especially after what had happened in the past two days. The laser mike wasn't doing much good either. It was limited to the west wing of the mansion, and they could train the beam on only one window at a time to pick up voices among the vibrations. It was hit or miss whether Gawbyan would be in the room of the window they chose.

The language barrier was another problem. Since neither man understood Burmese, they had no idea what was being discussed or who was speaking. Unless Maung Gawbyan was addressed by name or could be recognized by voiceprint identification, the taped conversations were useless. It didn't help that "Maung" seemed to be a fairly common name for Burmese. Several persons at the estate were addressed as such.

Bolan realized the button mikes might draw a blank if Gawbyan was afraid to discuss the heroin business in his office. If he was the slightest bit suspicious that someone had surreptitiously entered his office—the Executioner assumed the guy already suspected he had broken into the place because of Gawbyan's crooked deals—the diplomat wouldn't say a word about the heroin operation and would only discuss the most prosaic matters possible until he could have the office swept for bugs.

The Executioner and Gadgets Schwarz sat in the back of the van and waited for a translation of the button mike conversations to come back from Kurtzman's computer complex. It was the old "hurry up and wait" syndrome every soldier was familiar with.

"You never told me what the results were from those recordings I took at the Golden Lotus," Bolan said.

"I didn't get a chance to finish working on it," Schwarz replied. "Frankly it was a bigger chore than

I expected. Trying to separate voices speaking three or four languages all cluttered together was a real mess. I couldn't manage to get clear voiceprint IDs on anyone. So we sent the tape to the FBI. They have people who specialize in that kind of acoustics-segregation magic.''

The fax machine in the van suddenly came to life, sheets of dot-matrix print pouring into the tray. Kurtzman and his computers had come through again. The English translations of the Burmese conversations had arrived.

Bolan started to read the transcripts and most of the information was useless. Gawbyan complained that a cook had prepared breakfast wrong, that a servant hadn't shined the shoes he left outside his door and the maid had failed to dust the bookcase. Of slightly more interest was the fact that Gawbyan was clearing out his desk and getting ready to go to the airport. The Burmese delegation wanted him out of there as quickly as possible.

At last Bolan found what he was looking for. Gawbyan had a discussion with two subordinates. One man was concerned about the break-in and asked if it could have been associated with the heroin operation. Gawbyan didn't know, but he assured the others they had no reason to worry. He was going back to Myanmar and no one would suspect them. They would be safe to sell the rest of the heroin after he left.

One man expressed doubt about doing business with the Chinese. He complained about the Triad's poor security. Gawbyan said the robbery attempt at the Golden Lotus restaurant had been a fluke. Kwoon had arranged for another buy at a west-end pier. He explained that they had to get rid of the remaining heroin anyway. It was too risky to keep it hidden at the present location. Bolan wished they would have mentioned where that location was.

Gawbyan also reminded the other men that they needed to sell the remaining heroin to make a profit on this trip. Colonel Thaung would be very unhappy if they didn't sell some of the drugs and returned to Myanmar empty-handed. The Triad was the only buyer that they could count on. Certainly there were other criminal networks willing to purchase the heroin. Even some that would pay millions for it, but Gawbyan didn't know how to get in contact. Better to stick with Kwoon and the Triad.

The diplomat assured his men that the heroin shipments would continue to flow into the United States while he was out of the country. Gawbyan also predicted he would be back in America within two months.

The Executioner handed the important parts of the transcripts to Schwarz. The Able Team wizard scanned them briefly.

"You knew Gawbyan wasn't acting alone?"

"I figured he must have had help. Too much heroin was involved for one man to hide on his own. Too many diplomatic pouches had to be used. Other members of the delegation would have become suspicious if all of them had been for Gawbyan or if someone else hadn't backed his explanations for so many deliveries."

"And when the aides covered for him, that suggested they were the accomplices?" Schwarz asked.

"And he might have others. He certainly has some in Myanmar. Colonel Thaung for one. Whatever position this Thaung has, he must be one hell of a big shot back home. Sounds like he's the head honcho of this whole heroin operation."

"And the dope is going to keep coming in, too. You were right, Mack. It's not over."

"It's just beginning."

5

"You want to go to Myanmar?" Brognola asked.

"It's the only way to shut down the heroin pipe-line, Hal," Bolan replied. "If it isn't cut off at the source, it will keep coming into this country in dip-lomatic pouches. I don't have to tell you what drug abuse is doing to this nation."

Brognola leaned back in his chair at the end of the conference table in the War Room of Stony Man Farm. "Yeah, I know the use of heroin is increasing out there. I also know only a small portion of it is coming from these Burmese lowlifes. Hell, poppy fields are found in at least six countries outside the Golden Triangle. Mexico, Turkey, a couple of places in the Middle East, a couple more in the Far East and probably a couple we don't even know about."

"We know about this one."

"Okay. Do it. But one thing you might not have considered. Myanmar isn't stable these days. The politics since the elections in 1989 are still shaky, and Uncle Sam doesn't have a hell of a lot of pull over there. CIA and NSA operations there seem to be pretty lame. Things happened when it was still known as Burma, and neither the Company nor NSA appeared to have had any idea what was going on.''

"It's going to be pretty tough to operate on my own in a country where I don't speak the language.''

"I'll see what I can do for a contact," Brognola said. "But I don't like the idea, Striker. If this Colonel Thaung is as powerful as Gawbyan thinks he is, you'll have trouble getting anywhere near him. You'll be on his turf and if he even suspects you're an enemy—''

"Yeah. I know the rules. I've been playing them long enough. A lot might depend on how I try to get close to him. I'll think about my options and try to come up with something workable.''

"Sure. Try not to get yourself killed, okay?''

AARON KURTZMAN ROLLED his chair to the coffeemaker. He didn't ask Bolan if he wanted a cup. The Bear's coffee was about as appealing as caffeine-laced tar. Kurtzman was used to it. He spent long hours at the computer terminals and seldom wasted precious time doing things as trivial as washing the coffeepot.

"You must have calluses on the lining of your stomach," Bolan said.

"Separates the men from the boys.''

Kurtzman placed a cup of the evil, black brew in a receptacle attached to the arm of his chair and rolled to the memory banks in the artifical-intelligence data center.

Sheets of paper vomited from a fax machine and Kurtzman hurried to retrieve the information. He glanced over the material and grunted. One sheet was a reproduction of a photograph. Bolan glanced over the computer whiz's shoulder at the stern, lean face in the picture. A military service cap was perched on the man's head.

"Colonel Thaung?" the Executioner asked.

"Yeah," the Bear replied. "Kala Thaung. He was still Major Thaung when the photo was taken, which was only two years ago. This dude is a high mucka-muck in the new regime in Myanmar. Better read it, Striker. It won't make you happy, but read it anyway."

"Thaung is second- or third-highest ranking officer in the Directorate of Defence Services Intelligence," Bolan said. "DDSI is the most powerful security branch in Myanmar."

"Keep reading. It gets worse."

The information was less than encouraging. The DDSI was a military agency, specializing in intelligence gathering and investigations of alleged "enemies of the state." Thaung had been one of the leading officers involved in rounding up hundreds of people for interrogation. Since the DDSI didn't require warrants to search homes and businesses, or to make arrests, Thaung had little trouble getting "suspects." Many confessed to treason or being part of armed insurgencies against the government of Myanmar. Others had disappeared and never been heard of again. Thaung was said to be adept at torture and occasionally handled such actions personally.

Little else was on file about Colonel Thaung. He was believed to be forty-one years old, although his age wasn't certain. He was a widower. Thaung's wife and only child were killed during a firefight between government troops and rebels in the spring of 1987. A grenade reportedly exploded close to Thaung's spouse and son. He was well educated and graduated from a military academy at the head of his class. He spoke at least four languages fluently, including English and Mandarin Chinese, and he had received praise and commendations when he was a junior officer for his success in recruiting new military personnel from Shan states of northeastern Burma. This suggested he was familiar with the region and probably had a working vocabulary in one or more local dialects.

An interesting man. Highly intelligent, a skilled organizer and leader who could inspire trust and loyalty from his men. Yet, Thaung was also capable of incredible cruelty and ruthless behavior. The death of his wife and son might have triggered this dark side to the colonel's personality. A very dangerous man, Bolan realized.

"Told you it wouldn't make you happy."

"Didn't come here to be happy," Bolan replied. "What's the other sheet about?"

"This is from a source in Thailand," Kurtzman said. "A resistance movement has formed to oppose the current government in Myanmar. One of the members worked as a cutout for the CIA a few years ago. Back then he was part of a resistance group opposed to the government of General Ne Win who ran Burma for twenty-six years. Fellow's name is Byu Lone.

"He's in Thailand?" Bolan asked.

"Yeah. He and some others are trying to raise money and buy weapons to eventually carry out an armed revolution against the government of Myanmar. He used to be with Camp 101, a training outfit of the pro-democracy freedom fighters back in 1988. The Company files show Lone speaks English, is intelligent and reliable and adept in martial arts."

"Sounds good," Bolan said. "Can we get him to act as my contact in Myanmar?"

"I don't think we'll have any trouble recruiting him. Of course, we'll have to come up with enough money to interest him. Lone is trying to get funds for a revolution. That's an expensive business."

"Get in touch with him through the Company contacts in Thailand," Bolan said. "Lone sounds like what I need—a native of Myanmar. If Lone isn't available, I want somebody with his qualifications or as close as possible."

"I'll get on it," Kurtzman said. "Now, we can get weapons and other gear to Lone through the Company agents at the U.S. Embassy in Bangkok. The embassy in Myanmar isn't a good idea."

"Since Lone will have to get the weapons across the border into Thailand," Bolan said, "better keep the hardware small and dependable. A Desert Eagle and smaller handgun. I may need something concealable. One of the compact, reliable 9 mms would do. A .38 Special, if that's all they can get. No smaller calibers."

"You're sticking your neck out pretty far on this one, Striker. Even if we can recruit Lone, you'll be largely on your own and there won't be a hell of a lot we can do if you get in trouble."

"I can't say I know exactly what I'm getting into," the Executioner said, "because I never know for sure. But it's what has to be done."

6

The prisoner hung from the bar, naked and helpless. His arms had been pulled back and his thumbs wired together. The man's weight pulled his armpits painfully across the beam. His head leaned forward, chin on his chest.

Colonel Kala Thaung examined the captive without emotion. Torture was a clinical matter. One employed pain to a subject's anatomy to achieve desired results. The prisoner's body was marked with numerous bruises and cuts. His face was battered and bloodied. His nose had been smashed, his lips were bleeding and swollen. His eyes were closed and sealed shut by the puffed, bruised flesh around the lids.

"You've been here for three days," the DDSI officer said. "Isn't that long enough? None of your friends would have gone through a single hour of this without telling us about you. Why don't you tell us about them?"

The psychology was intended to appeal to the prisoner's ego. By telling the man he had endured far greater punishment than his accomplices could have managed, Thaung hoped to convince him he wouldn't lose face by breaking down and giving the torturers names and addresses.

"Do...not...know...any..." the captive replied. He could barely speak because his lips and tongue were swollen.

"We found the literature in your home. It criticized the State Law and Order Restoration Council, the military and the police. What sort of country would Myanmar be without law and order? Without the military and the police to protect the people?"

He grabbed the prisoner's hair and yanked the man's head to one side, glaring at the beaten face as he spoke.

"You want anarchy?" he asked. "You fool! Citizens would be victims to every gang of roaming hoodlums that happened along. Do you want such thieves breaking into homes? Attacking innocent people on the street? Myanmar would be a jungle unfit for decent people."

The colonel jammed a thumb to the prisoner's crushed nose. He dug the nail deep and the captive screamed with pain. Thaung stepped back and swung a boot to the prisoner's unprotected genitals. The man moaned and passed out from the agony between his legs.

"You disgust me," Thaung said. "People like you have no values."

A soldier appeared at the cell door and announced that Colonel Myint was waiting to speak with Thaung on the telephone.

"Work on this one while I'm gone," the colonel ordered. "Throw water on him to revive him. Remind him next time he might get a blade in his manhood instead of a boot. We want to know where he got that subversive literature, who wrote it and who printed the copies."

"He might not know who wrote it and printed it, sir. The booklets were produced on a crude handmade press. You said it appeared the print type was made of clay, and anyone with some paper and ink could have made the copies."

"That's why we have to put an end to this immediately. If we don't stop it now, dozens more will emulate this traitor and print more criticism about the government. Finally no one will trust the state or have any faith in it. We cannot allow that to happen. It could wreck the morale of the entire nation."

"Yes, Colonel."

Thaung left the cell block. The warden stood by the open door to his office. He let the colonel enter and moved away so the man couldn't accuse him of trying to eavesdrop on the conversation. Thaung moved to the desk. The receiver to the telephone was off the hook and lay on an ink blotter. He picked it up.

"This is Thaung. I am always eager to speak with any member of our State Law and Order Restoration Council, Colonel Myint."

"Maung Gawbyan is on his way back from the United States. You know he was accused of smuggling heroin into the American city of New York? They say he was trying to sell it to gangsters."

"That cannot be true," Thaung replied. "I know Gawbyan personally. I even helped him get his position as a diplomat."

"I noticed that in Gawbyan's record," the SLORC official replied. "That's why I thought I should talk to you."

"I understand. Of course Maung Gawbyan isn't a smuggler. It's too soon to speak without knowing all the facts, but I suspect that what happened in America is that some of our enemies fabricated this story as an effort to embarrass Myanmar. The Americans have been critical of our country ever since we took control from the tyrant General Win."

"You think the Americans are looking for a scapegoat? They're attempting to blame us for their drug problem?"

"Isn't that typical of them?" Thaung asked. "They claimed Noriega was involved in the cocaine traffic and money-laundering operations. They still have a problem with cocaine use in the United States. They blame this on Colombia or Bolivia. Yankees used heroin in the past and they blamed this on Turkey for having poppy fields. Some even blamed China. They said it was the fault of the Chinese for introducing opium dens to America."

"That's a ridiculous claim," Myint said. "Don't they know poppies didn't even exist in China until the Portuguese brought them and starting growing the opium flowers in the seventeenth century? The British got involved in the opium trade in the eighteenth century. Chinese emperors tried to stop the traffic, especially the opium coming into their country. The British were so determined to trade in opium, they actually went to war against China to do so. Haven't the Americans ever heard of the Opium Wars?"

"Perhaps they don't share your enthusiasm for history," Thaung suggested.

Myint didn't respond. The silence told Thaung he had overplayed his effort to appeal to Myint's favorite topic. Thaung knew the SLORC officer was a historian and liked to slip into abbreviated lectures on the subject. However, Myint had apparently realized Thaung had encouraged this to direct the discussion from Gawbyan.

"If someone has been smuggling heroin into the United States by using our diplomatic pouches we'd better find out," Myint said. "When Gawbyan arrives we should question him. You're very good at getting the truth from people. You've convinced more than two hundred people to confess to treason, crimes against the state. Of course, some of them committed suicide from a sense of guilt. Isn't that correct?"

"That has happened."

"Incredible how so many of your prisoners actually beat themselves to death. Do they smash their own heads into walls repeatedly?"

"I don't have any of the reports of individual interrogations with me at this time," Thaung said. "My memory is lacking a bit on details because I haven't dealt with many interrogations in the past year. Not directly. Working liaison with other departments does have me involved in supervision on occasion."

"That's what you're doing at Insein Prison today?"

"The People's Police Force arrested some subversives and they wound up here. DDSI is dedicated to finding such enemies of our country and gathering information from them that will help us locate other traitors. I'm just doing my job, Colonel."

"I know," Myint said. "You put so much effort into your work. Because you are an expert, you might supervise the interrogation of Maung Gawbyan."

"I am confident he isn't a traitor, but I suppose we have to be certain."

"We have to find out the truth about this. Regardless of who might be involved. Heroin trafficking and cultivating opium poppies is a very serious matter."

"True. Yet, we don't have proof this is happening in Myanmar. The accusations by the Americans may be a total falsehood."

"I hope you're right, Colonel Thaung."

When Myint hung up, Thaung slammed the phone receiver into the cradle. The SLORC officer planned to make things difficult. Thaung would have to prepare for any trouble Myint had in mind.

He stepped from the office. A soldier met him in the hallway.

"Colonel, the prisoner we were interrogating is dead."

"Dead?" Thaung repeated. "The prisoner downstairs? How did he die?"

"We revived him with some water as you instructed," the soldier said. "Interrogation began, and I applied a wire loop to his genitals."

"You shouldn't have used that method," Thaung said. "It can throw a man into shock, and sometimes the subject swallows his own tongue and chokes to death on it. Is that was happened?''

The soldier nodded, shamefaced.

''Report his death as a suicide,'' the colonel ordered.

7

When Jason Kwoon became a member of the Hwang Shui Triad he had to participate in an initiation ritual at the society's secret lodge. It was a very old tradition, and Kwoon wasn't certain what some of the trappings of the ritual represented. The lodge had been filled with incense, pictures and flags hung on the walls. A chicken had been decapitated and its blood mixed with some wine.

The Chief Incense Burner, a high-ranking member of the Triad and master of the quasimystical ceremonies of the society, then pricked Kwoon's finger with a knife and his blood was added to the wine as well. All present drank this odd mixture, and the Incense Chief told Kwoon it was time for him to swear his oaths of loyalty to the Hwang Shui. He recited the oaths. There were more than thirty of them. He had to promise not to betray the society, not to steal from fellow Triad members or commit adultery with their wives or even think about such things. The list went on and on. After each oath, Kwoon had to declare that he would be killed by "many swords" or "bolts of lightning" if he failed to keep his vow.

Kwoon wasn't concerned about being struck by lightning or stabbed to death by swords. He figured those would be mercifully swift compared to what his fellow Triad members would do to him if anything went wrong with the heroin deal that night. He and Maung Gawbyan had escaped with their lives when the shooting occurred at the Golden Lotus restaurant. However, the other Triad hardmen present had been killed. This made his brethren suspicious about Kwoon's good fortune since he had arranged the meeting with the Burmese diplomat.

Yet, the Shan Ling-Shou, the leader of the Triad society, had personally decided to give Kwoon another chance to make the heroin buy. The Hwang Shui wasn't as large as many of the other Triads, and it needed new sources of heroin to compete with the criminal organizations in New York. One was either a tiger or a wolf in the world of crime. The wolf may be feared, but the tiger will consume him if their paths cross. The Hwang Shui couldn't be a tiger unless it could increase its supply of heroin.

Gawbyan had been called back to Myanmar, but two of his aides were supposed to meet Kwoon at the pier. He didn't intend to let anything go wrong this time. Kwoon was accompanied by six enforcers, known as Hong Kan or Red Poles. They were trained in *wu-shu,* traditional martial arts, and they also carried firearms and knives. Four Red Poles were strategically positioned at the harbor to act as lookouts and to take out anyone who even appeared to be a threat. The other two enforcers remained by Kwoon's side.

He wasn't taking any chances of being outdone by firepower as had happened at the restaurant when the mysterious man showed up with an Uzi. Kwoon carried a Swedish-made M-45 submachine gun with a 36-round magazine in the well. Similar in design to the old Nazi MP-40 "Schmeisser," the M-45 was a blowback action, full-automatic weapon that spit out 600 rounds per minute.

Dense fog drifted across the pier and caressed the Triad hardmen with a clammy embrace. City lights were blurred by the fog, and the surrounding warehouses and docked boats appeared strange and shadowy. Kwoon was getting nervous. If the Burmese chickened out or decided to sell the dope to somebody else, Kwoon would have their heads mounted on the wall in his den. He probably wouldn't get the chance to go after them, though, he realized. If the deal went sour, the Red Poles might turn on him.

A pair of headlights stabbed the darkness. It was another big black sedan. The Burmese diplomatic vehicle rolled to a halt, and Kwoon recognized Gawbyan's aides as they emerged from the car.

"You're late," Kwoon said. He spoke English, unsure if the Burmese understood Chinese.

"The fog slowed us down," an aide replied. "We brought the merchandise. You have the money?"

"Let's see the white stuff first."

One Burmese walked to the rear of the sedan, unlocked the trunk and unlocked four suitcases nestled inside.

Kwoon stared down at the plastic bags filled with heroin. Ninety kilos approximate total, he thought.

Pure horse. After it was cut and prepared for the street, the Triad would have about four hundred kilos. The profit potential was staggering. It might be worth as much as half a billion dollars.

"The money, Mr. Kwoon," a Burmese prodded.

"Of course. We had agreed three and half million dollars. However, since you lost your first shipment, which must have been a disappointment, we decided to express our goodwill. The payment will now be four million."

The Burmese were delighted with this news and Kwoon almost laughed in their beaming, happy faces. They were getting ripped off and were too dumb to know it. Heroin in Southeast Asia could be sold for a decent profit by Burmese standards, but the shit was worth nearly a hundred thousand times as much in NYC. Four million dollars? The Triad would have gladly paid twenty, and they still would have come out way ahead of the game.

Red Poles hefted out baggage from a rented U-Haul. The cases were filled with cash in twenty-dollar bills. The Burmese looked at the money with astonishment. They came from a poor country where the average annual income was the equivalent of $220. The aides were well paid by Burmese standards, yet they didn't earn as much in a year as a single stack of bills in the cases.

"It is a great honor to do business with you," a Burmese said, bowing to Kwoon. "I hope we shall be able to do much more trade in the future."

"That is also the wish of the Hwang Shui Triad," Kwoon replied.

"None of you will get what you want," said a graveyard voice from the fog.

Kwoon grabbed his M-45 and swung the barrel in the general direction he thought the voice had come from. Dammit! What happened to the Red Pole who was supposed to have the area covered? How many guys were out there? Just one, or was the pier surrounded by cops and Feds?

The enforcers unsheathed pistols. One dashed to the U-Haul and reached for a shotgun. The Burmese jumped behind the sedan for cover and drew the small-caliber autoloaders they carried for general self-defense. Kwoon knelt by some crates and fired a short burst, hoping to draw the enemy into returning fire. The muzzle-flash could betray the guy's position and give Kwoon a decent idea where the hell to place the next salvo.

MACK BOLAN WATCHED the traffickers scurry about the pier. He knelt alongside a warehouse, three hundred yards away. The corpse of a Red Pole lay in the shadows nearby.

The Executioner had been hiding in the building more than an hour before the Triad hardmen arrived. He waited for the Burmese to deliver the goods before he crept outside and took out the Triad sentry. Bolan had throttled the man with a "commando steel sling," well aware he had to do the Red Pole quickly or try to go one-on-one with the Kung Fu-trained sentry in hand-to-hand combat.

Bolan had fought Triad hardmen before. They were better with their martial arts than firearms, so he didn't intend to fight them on their terms if he could avoid it. Like every good military strategist, Bolan hadn't come unprepared for the situation. He had anticipated the fog would be heavy and this would be in his favor.

The warrior carried an M-16 assault rifle with an infrared night scope mounted to the frame. The special night-vision optics in the lens turned the darkest night, or the foggiest, into mere dusk. Since it magnified reflected light on objects, the Starlite was better than infrared—no blinding glare from a burst of sudden bright light or the muzzle-flash of one's own weapon.

He looked through the scope. The figures appeared to be ghostly shapes in the yellow and green world viewed through the lens. Kwoon was trying to sucker him into revealing his position. The Triad gunners were armed with pistols and one shotgun. No sweat as long as Bolan was out of effective range. However, he hadn't located one of the Red Pole sentries and that was an unknown factor that worried him. The Burmese were probably the least threatening of the lot, but the warrior knew better than to underestimate them. If they got cornered, the aides would fight, and they hadn't drawn fountain pens from their jackets.

Kwoon was armed with the most firepower and was therefore the logical first target. Bolan aimed with care and centered the cross hairs on Kwoon's forehead. When the hardman rose to trigger another volley, the Executioner squeezed the trigger. A trio of

5.56 mm slugs erupted from the M-16, drilling into Kwoon's head and taking him out of play.

The man with the shotgun unleashed a burst of buckshot when he glimpsed the muzzle-flash of the M-16. Pellets struck a Dumpster a hundred yards from Bolan's position. The shotgunner repeated the action, and Bolan realized the man was neither stubborn nor stupid. He was trying to distract the Executioner while two of his pistol-packing cronies tried to move closer. They knew they were out of range and hoped to get within effective firing distance with their handguns.

Bolan aimed for the closest opponent and fired another 3-round burst. The M-16 slugs stabbed into the Triad gunner's chest left of the center and he went down. The other Red Poles leaped for cover, aware that their strategy had failed.

The warrior saw movement via the corner of an eye. He whirled to discover the missing Triad enforcer had circled the area and attempted to close in, his .357 Magnum up and ready. Bolan snap-aimed and triggered a short salvo. The guy stopped the bullets with his torso. He fell back and fired his S&W wheel gun, but the slug streaked harmlessly into the night sky.

The shotgun roared, and buckshot peppered the ground twenty yards from Bolan. The remaining Red Poles were on the move again. They had taken advantage of Bolan being occupied with their comrade in order to draw closer to his position. Another load of double-ought buckshot landed even closer as Bolan ducked by the edge of the warehouse.

The Triad gunners would probably attempt a fork attack to try to get him in a cross fire, the warrior guessed. He moved to the opposite corner and found a hardman creeping through the fog. Bolan braced the stock of the assault rifle against a hip and opened fire. His enemy stopped in midstride and staggered back several steps. He raised his pistol, but it slipped from his fingers and he collapsed to his knees, no longer able to stand. The man glanced down at the bloodstains on his shirt as if surprised to realize he had been shot. Then he fell face forward onto the ground.

The Executioner quickly turned his attention to the side of the warehouse where the remaining Red Pole opponent was located. He risked a careful look around the corner and saw that the surviving Red Pole was frantically trying to feed shells into the tubular magazine of his shotgun. The guy was only three yards away, but he had also burned up the ammo in his weapon.

The growl of a car engine told Bolan his other quarry was getting away. As the warrior snapped off a quick shot to take out the Triad gunner, the sedan rocketed forward.

Bolan ran to the driveway and drew his Beretta 93-R, the headlights filling his vision as he jogged into the path of the charging vehicle.

He saw the windshield above the glare, recognized the silhouette of a man's head and shoulders and triggered the Beretta. A trio of 9 mm parabellums spit from the muzzle. The warrior glimpsed spiderweb cracks in the windshield an instant before he leaped to one side.

The sedan rocketed past Bolan, but it didn't get far. The car crashed into a cargo crane, the fender and hood crumpling on impact. Steam hissed from the ruptured radiator. Bolan jogged to the vehicle and wrenched open the front passenger door. The Burmese inside wouldn't be running dope anymore. Both had been killed on impact.

8

"Geez," Inspector Michael O'Hara said, "is this some kind of new trend?"

"What's that, sir?" a patrolman asked.

"Nothing. Just thinking out loud."

O'Hara knew he should not jump to conclusions, but he was already sure the scene at the pier was somehow related to the carnage that occurred in Chinatown two nights earlier. There were some differences. They had found nine bodies at the pier, two less than at the Golden Lotus, and there'd been no wounded bystanders either. He wasn't sure any of the dead at the pier had been innocent. O'Hara hoped not. He didn't really give a damn if criminals wanted to kill one another.

Even then, he would have to investigate. That was what homicide cops did. They looked at dead bodies and tried to figure out how it happened and who did it. O'Hara had seen a lot of dead people since he had joined the force, but he had never come across two scenes of extraordinary violence within less than seventy-two hours. These weren't homicide scenes. They were battlefields.

O'Hara took out a pack of cigarettes as he leaned against the rear fender of a squad car. The area had been cordoned off as a police investigation site, though there weren't many rubberneckers hanging around the docks at three o'clock in the morning. The press would be there in a little while and O'Hara didn't feel like talking to them. He just didn't know what to say.

"Hey, Mike!" a voice called out. "What the hell is going on here lately?"

O'Hara glanced up as Jeff Greene approached with a couple of his men. Greene was narcotics division, and they encountered each other frequently. Drugs and death went together like ham and cheese. However, O'Hara was surprised to see that Greene had already arrived at the scene.

"You got here quick," O'Hara said. "Who called you?"

"An anonymous tip that there was a shitload of heroin in a car down here. I thought it was a crock at first. Sounded like somebody read the paper or heard the news about the incident in Chinatown and made up a story based on that."

"The car is over there, Jeff," O'Hara said. "Another black sedan. This one had a little accident after somebody shot his face off."

"Another big black sedan," Greene said. "This isn't another diplomat's car from the Burma embassy, is it?"

"You mean the UN delegation from Myanmar. And yes, that's exactly what it is."

"This is nuts. Is there some sort of gang war going on?"

"I never knew a gang war where they left millions of dollars worth of dope behind," O'Hara said dryly. "You ever see that since you've been in narcotics?"

"Never even heard of it before. This is Chinatown again, right?"

"Yeah," O'Hara replied. "There's a connection, but I don't know what. We got Chinese gang members here of some sort. Maybe Tong or I think they call them Triad these days."

"Don't even mention them," Green warned. "My boss says they don't exist. Says if we mention that word to the press he'll have us on foot patrol in Harlem. He claims the Chinese community could consider it to be a disparaging remark that would cast them in a poor light."

"Sure. Triads don't exist, and neither does the Mafia or the Colombian cartels. If we pretend organized crime families don't exist, they'll just go away."

Greene glanced at the bullet-ravaged corpses of two slain Chinese. Another body lay by the car and a fourth was still inside the vehicle.

"Looks like a few of them have been put away for keeps. How many are there?"

"Nine," O'Hara replied. "I'm not sure how many dudes hit these suckers. I'd think it would have to be at least three or four. Damn well-trained marksmen too. Well-armed with automatic rifles. One guy here got strangled with a wire. Commando-style. Another one I'm not sure what happened to him. Looks like he has a broken neck."

"There were no witnesses?"

"Sure. Whoever took these guys out saw what happened. What about the tip you got on the phone? You record it? Maybe we can get a voiceprint."

"Nope. Whoever called used an electronic hand-kerchief."

"Is that a joke?" O'Hara asked.

"No. It's for real. It's a device you can use to cover a phone receiver and speak into it. The gizmo distorts the caller's voice and renders its voiceprint useless. Pretty fancy equipment for thugs to be using."

"You'd be surprised what thugs can get hold of these days. Still, that sounds more like some sort of spy contraption. Sort of thing the CIA might use."

"Why the hell would an espionage agency ambush a bunch of dope dealers and leave the heroin? Figure that's their hobby?"

"I don't know what to think," O'Hara admitted. "That thing in Chinatown looked like a robbery attempt and some Chinese hoods happened to be there and it turned into a shootout. The strangest part about that was some witnesses said there was a tall guy there who seemed to be fighting both the Chinese gang members and the punkers. A mother and father swore the guy saved their kid when one of the low-life jerks was about to blast him."

"Are you thinking he was some kind of street vigilante who just happened to be in the area and was packing an Uzi?"

O'Hara shrugged.

"Well," Greene said, "I'd better get that heroin and take it back so the lab can run some tests. That first batch from the other night turned out to be pure, uncut Chinese White. If this turns out to be the same, the chances the two incidents were connected goes up, pal."

"Chinese White?" O'Hara asked.

"Yeah. There's different types of heroin. Makes a difference where it's from and how it's been processed. There's Turkish White and Mexican Brown, both of which are powder form and shot up with needles. But there are two kinds of Chinese heroin. Chinese Brown is sort of a chunky, shitty type, almost always smoked. Can't shoot it up. Chinese White, on the other hand, is usually considered to be the most valuable and desirable brand of heroin available."

"I understand," O'Hara said. "But this Chinese White doesn't necessarily come from China, does it? I mean don't they grow the shit in places like Vietnam and Thailand?"

"Well, not Vietnam necessarily, but they do have poppy fields in Laos and Thailand and . . . Burma."

"So maybe this Chinese White is actually Burmese dope and the guys from the delegation were selling it to the New York Triads," O'Hara said.

"This would be a good place for a buy," Greene said. "You find any money?"

"No," O'Hara replied. "Maybe whoever hit these bastards just wanted the cash and took off with it. Probably be a lot of money."

"Millions, man. Sure is a logical reason to waste nine guys who aren't anything but trash anyway. But why the hell would the people who did it call the department and tell us where to pick up the dope?"

"I guess they didn't want to take the chance the drugs could fall into the hands of other criminals," O'Hara suggested. "Maybe our boy is civic-minded."

"Our boy? You talk as if one guy did this."

"Figure of speech," O'Hara replied. "No way just one man could have done this job."

He hoped he sounded convincing, because he wasn't sure what he said was true.

FATHER TONY WOKE shortly after dawn. He climbed from his cot and began the morning with a prayer, asking God to help him keep the Room at His Inn from having to shut down. The place was a shelter for the homeless in New York. Father Tony had struggled for years to get the funds to build it to help the poor, wretched souls so badly in need of a decent lodging away from the hostile streets and the crushing poverty and despair.

The priest had dedicated his life to helping the homeless. His shelter had been more successful in some ways than most because he weeded out the drug addicts, alcoholics and mentally ill people from the other poor. Not that Father Tony sent these individuals back to the streets to fend for themselves. He tried to get the junkies into rehab centers, and the alcoholics had to enroll in AA or some other sort of self-help group. If they agreed and genuinely tried to kick the dope or booze, they could stay at the shelter.

The mentally ill persons had to meet with psychological consulors. Those who needed medication were taken to free clinics for help. Few were violent, but Tony could not allow them among the others. He was trying to do more than give people room and shelter. The priest did his best to help them find work or complete schooling so they could qualify for a job-training program.

So many people had seen their hopes and dreams dashed in recent years. Families were torn apart. Some had been evicted from their homes with nowhere to go but the streets. Some were young runaways who had no home to return to except one of abuse and mistreatment. Many were women with one or more children. No wonder so many homeless turned to alcohol or drugs, the priest thought.

Now, Father Tony saw his efforts about to go down the drain. The funds were no longer coming in, and he couldn't afford to keep the shelter open. Room at His Inn wasn't receiving support from the government on any level. Father Tony hadn't wanted to take taxpayers' money. He had hoped that the goodwill and charity of his congregation, the people of New York and the visitors to the city would be enough to finance the shelter. However, the funds had dwindled in the past two years. Perhaps the recession and fear of the economy going into a tailspin, higher taxes or the exposure of certain charities that raised money only to line the pockets of the people running them had discouraged the public from supporting the shelter.

Father Tony finished his prayers and prepared for another day's work. His duties started in the morning and continued until after sundown. The priest was involved with everything from preparations of meals, laundry, classes in reading for children—and some adults—to spiritual advice, religious services and listening to confessions. He also had to write sermons and prepare for three services at the church every week as well. Not an easy work load for a man approaching sixty, but Father Tony accepted the burden gladly because he never felt that he had done more good for his fellow human beings than with the shelter. How better to serve God than to follow the most basic principle of love thy neighbor?

"Good morning, Father," Elena greeted. "I got you tea, toast and eggs. You gonna eat breakfast today, too."

Elena was the shelter's den mother. The priest smiled. She fretted over him and constantly nagged Tony about not eating enough or getting adequate rest. Elena was as devoted to the shelter as Tony. What a pity it was almost over. He hadn't had the heart to tell her they would have to close down.

The priest followed her into the kitchen. Breakfast was on the table and he was surprised to see a large cardboard box there, as well. Wrapped in brown paper and bound with string, the package bore Father Tony's name and the address of the shelter. He asked Elena where it came from.

"A kid on a bike dropped it off a few minutes ago. He said he was on his way to school when a man asked him if he could deliver it. The kid said the man claimed there was something in the box you might need. I think the guy must have paid the kid to deliver it 'cause he looked pretty happy."

"Let's see what it is."

Father Tony used a table knife to cut away the string and paper. No doubt it was a donation of clothes or blankets or food. Although he appreciated such generosity and realized many people couldn't afford to give more, the supplies for the shelter would do little good after he had to close the doors....

"My Lord," the priest breathed. "Is this real or am I dreaming?"

The box was filled with stacks of twenty-dollar bills. The shelter needed close to a hundred thousand dollars to stay in business. There was more than that in the box. Four or five times that much. Elena stared down at the money and whispered something in Spanish. She clutched the crucifix and said, *"Gracias."*

Father Tony found a note with the cash and read it aloud.

"'I know about your work. You've done good things. Heard you have some money trouble. Hope this helps so you can keep doing good things.' It appears to be written with a laundry marker and there is no signature."

"It is a miracle, Father," Elena said.

"But I don't know where this money came from."

"You know how you can use it. Do like the letter says. 'Keep doing good things.'"

9

Maung Gawbyan sat across the desk from Colonel Myint, feeling uncomfortable. The State Law and Order Restoration Council was the highest military authority in Myanmar. This position, and the fact Myint was a senior ranking officer, placed his authority above Colonel Thaung.

"These accusations of dealing in heroin smuggling and attempted sale of the drugs to American gangsters deeply disturbs us," Myint said. "I know you claim to be innocent of these charges, but you haven't explained how your car was found with a large amount of heroin in the trunk."

"I believe the explanation is in my report," Gawbyan replied.

Myint leafed through some papers on his desk. He smiled without mirth and glanced up at Thaung. The DDSI officer stood at the opposite side of the room, and his expression seemed as calm as a face of stone.

"You've read this?" Myint asked. "And you believe it, Colonel?"

"I do," Thaung replied. "However, I don't believe the heroin was planted in the car by the American criminals. I suspect the drugs were in the trunk prior to the gun battle at the Chinese restaurant.''

Gawbyan stared at Thaung. The colonel appeared to be in the process of betraying him and leaving him at the mercy of Myint and the SLORC.

"So you believe the heroin was smuggled into the United States in our diplomatic pouches?'' Myint inquired.

"Absolutely,'' Thaung replied. "However, it wasn't done by Maung Gawbyan. His aides were responsible. They were the drug smugglers. The most recent report from our delegation states that the two aides to Maung Gawbyan were killed in some sort of gang violence in New York City. Their bodies were found with several slain individuals believed to be members of a Chinese Triad society operating in the city. Ninety kilos of heroin were also found in the vehicle the aides had driven to the scene.''

"I am aware of that report,'' Myint said. "But, I find it difficult to believe Maung Gawbyan didn't know his aides were involved in drug activities. Diplomatic pouches weren't addressed to them, but he was receiving such packages. Correct?''

"My duties at the United Nations consumed most of my time, Colonel Myint,'' Gawbyan said, playing along with the story Thaung had fabricated. "I didn't have an opportunity to check the pouches and left this task to my aides. They might have even used my name when contacting persons in Myanmar to have such packages delivered. There is no way I could know what evil deeds they might have been involved with.''

"You must have very poor judgment to have such individuals on your staff," Myint said. "Or did you select them, Colonel? I notice those aides were members of the DDSI."

"You are right," Thaung replied. "Poor judgment on my part. However, Maung Gawbyan is innocent. His only crime is too much dedicated concentration to his duties as our diplomat and too much trust in the people I had assigned him as his aides and personal security."

Myint didn't believe their story, and his expression revealed this. The SLORC officer's eyes burned with anger. He knew they were lying. He couldn't prove it, but they would have a difficult chore proving their story to be true.

"We'll investigate this matter in greater detail," Myint said. "I want to find out who was responsible for the shipment of the pouches from Yangon."

"I'll begin the investigation immediately," Thaung declared.

"It would probably be better if someone else headed this investigation," Myint replied. "Someone who isn't associated with the case. You are a friend of Maung Gawbyan, and the men suspected of smuggling were members of the DDSI. Instead, I believe we'll have another agency look into this. You are a liaison officer with the People's Police Force and the Special Investigation Department, correct?"

Thaung confirmed this."

"Then we'll have the Criminal Investigation Department deal with the case. We really have too many security agencies for a country less than 700,000 square kilometers and with a population of less than thirty-seven million."

"As an officer in the SLORC you certainly appreciate the need for enforcement of law and order," Gawbyan said.

"To maintain law and order is necessary," Myint replied. "But I don't want to see Myanmar follow the path set down by General Win and the Burma Socialist Program Party. We had twenty-six years of that tyrant and his oppression. Our new order has to be a genuine improvement. It must be better than what we tore down in 1988."

"It is better," Thaung said. "But we still have enemies."

"Yes," Myint replied. "I know."

COLONEL MYINT WAS still furious an hour after Thaung and Gawbyan left his office. He was certain they were involved in a conspiracy to produce and sell heroin for profit. However, they were powerful men, especially Thaung. The Directorate of Defence Services Intelligence was second only to the SLORC itself in authority in Myanmar. It was also gaining more power and influence. Worse, most members of the SLORC thought the DDSI was doing a wonderful job and Kala Thaung was a superb example of why it worked so well.

Colonel Kala Thaung was a brutal opportunist and torturer. He had built his list of "enemies of the state" who he had "discovered" by forcing confessions from the pour souls he arrested and tormented with devices of pain. Thaung was ambitious and brutal. Myint believed the man was capable of any evil in his quest for wealth and power.

So little had changed since Burma became Myanmar, Myint thought sadly. The same vicious tactics were being used since the revolution. His country could never be a respected and admired nation until the politics of terror came to an end. Myint loved his country. It was rich in history that dated back to 3000 B.C., and Burma-Myanmar had survived the occupation of the Mongols, the British, and the Japanese military during World War II. After enduring so much for so long, Myint believed his country deserved more than to be a backward police state.

Men like Thaung and Gawbyan were part of the problem. Myint was determined to see that they didn't escape paying for their crimes. He called the Criminal Investigation Department and demanded to see its top officer immediately. Fifty minutes later the man hadn't arrived at Myint's office. He called the CID twice and was told the investigator had been contacted and would soon be at the colonel's office. He reached for the phone to call once more.

Glass shattered, and Myint turned to stare at a projectile as it hit the floor. The colonel glimpsed the short piece of pipe, capped at both ends. He didn't need to see the sputtering fuse to realize it was a pipe bomb. Myint dropped behind his desk.

· The bomb exploded with tremendous force. The desk was reduced to splinters and Colonel Myint was ripped apart by flying shards of wood and metal. His office was destroyed and the door blasted from its hinges. A second pipe bomb sailed through the window and exploded with a charge of white phosphorous, engulfing the room in flames.

COLONEL THAUNG HEARD the explosion, like thunder in the distance, as he sat in a small restaurant. He sipped tea calmly and waited for Lieutenant Po to report. The junior officer arrived a few minutes later and joined Thaung at the table.

"Our man on the telephone box intercepted Myint's calls," Po explained. "He pretended to be a CID clerk. Colonel Myint called back twice, so he never suspected his phone line wasn't going through to the Criminal Investigation Department."

"And the explosions?" Thaung asked. "Are you certain Myint was in his office when the pipe grenades were launched?"

"Yes, Colonel. Captain Lat saw Myint quite clearly from the rooftop before he fired the first bomb. We used crude pipe devices, as you instructed, launched from a shotgun converted into a grenade launcher. Of course, the explosives were far more powerful than those commonly used for such primitive bombs. The white phosphorous should burn up ample evidence of this."

"As well as any note that Myint may have had concerning Gawbyan or myself," Thaung said. "And the rebel 'assassins' have been brought to justice?"

"Of course," Po answered. "Luckily Captain Lat and Sergeant Gyi got to the roof before the rebels could escape. Too bad they had to kill the murderers and they can't tell us who sent them to assassinate Colonel Myint."

Po smiled as he spoke. Two suspected members of a students' democratic reform movement had been taken up to the rooftop by Captain Lat and Sergeant Gyi. Handcuffed and gagged, they watched helplessly while Lat fired the pipe bombs. Then, it was a simple matter to wait a few minutes, while confusion reigned in the streets and SLORC headquarters, before killing the two students. The shotgun launcher was planted in the hands of one corpse and a handgun placed beside the other.

"I hope the handcuffs weren't put on too tightly," Thaung said. "If it left marks, some might become suspicious."

"I was with the captain and sergeant when they picked up the student troublemakers," Po replied. "We were careful, Colonel. Besides, the SLORC will be outraged by this rebel attack and grateful to the Directorate of Defense Services Intelligence for rescuing them from further terrorism. Captain Lat and Sergeant Gyi will certainly be heroes for thinking so quickly and taking such prompt action."

"You've done your job well, Lieutenant," Thaung said. "I'll speak with the captain and sergeant personally before the night is over. Their role will receive the most public attention, but your part was equally important. I won't forget that."

"I'll take a promotion and larger payment from our business instead of medals and public praise," Po assured him.

"You'd better go now," Thaung said. "Inform Gawbyan that we've taken care of Colonel Myint. Tell him to relax. The government is going to be far too concerned about threats from internal guerilla groups to be terribly concerned about a possible scandal in the United States. With Myint out of the way, the others will eagerly accept the theory that Gawbyan's aides were the only heroin smugglers involved in that sordid affair.''

"The real pity is we lost a hundred and eighty kilos and didn't make a single kyat in the process. The deal with that Triad in the United States was supposed to earn us almost forty-six and a half million kyat.''

''I know. We have to establish a new pipeline into the West. They have a greater appetite for drugs in the United States than anywhere else in the world. They're also willing to pay the most for their habit. It is vital we establish trade there if we want to make truly large profits.''

"That might take some time now."

"Perhaps, but we have to find a way. The longer it takes, the more difficult to establish a firm foothold in America. Others are involved in dealing heroin to the United States. It will be harder to peddle our goods there if the supply is flooding in from other sources. Besides, drug use in America seems to follow strange trends. Five years ago the use of heroin by Americans had dropped and the majority favored cocaine. Now, heroin has increased in America, but that trend could change in another year.''

"It may take that long for us to build another pipeline."

"No," Thaung insisted. "There has to be a way."

10

The trip to Myanmar was long, and the route wasn't direct from Washington, D.C. to Rangoon. Bolan's flight had taken him to Istanbul, Turkey, where he boarded a Myanmar Airways Corporation plane. The view of Myanmar from the air was magnificent. Tropical forests covered much of the country, and great mountains formed a mighty horseshoe pattern around the abundance of exotic green.

As the plane flew above Mandalay, at the center of Myanmar, Bolan gazed down at a fabulous array of Buddhist shrines. The pagodas appeared to be carved of ivory, the white stone and marble beautifully crafted. Conical domes stood tall along the hills, some capped with stunning golden steeples.

It seemed difficult to imagine such a beautiful country, with graceful shrines and Buddhist monasteries, could be a brutal police state. However, Bolan was aware of the reality that Myanmar had a dark side. The country might have deserved its title "the Land of Golden Pagodas," but it was also part of the Golden Triangle, a hub of drug activity and corruption on every level.

The plane approached Rangoon and descended to the airport. The view of the capital city looked intriguing. There was another plethora of beautiful domes and steeples to Buddhist shrines, relatively few large modern buildings and a lot of smaller dwellings teeming with activity that appeared to be marketplaces from a distance.

In the airport customs didn't even ask to look in his carryon. He could have been smuggling in plutonium warheads and they wouldn't have known. Bolan carried his small black duffel bag to the baggage area. He discovered his other case had been lost, which didn't surprise the warrior. The baggage manager spoke English and apologized for the inconvenience. He promised the suitcase would be sent to "Mr. Michael Belasko's" room as soon as it arrived. Bolan explained that he would be staying at the Martaban Hotel.

Outside, the American was accosted by beggars, street merchants and cabdrivers. He picked the cabbie who seemed to have the best grasp of English, the other drivers reluctantly backing off as Bolan followed the chosen man to his taxi. The car as a battered heap, at least twenty years old. Bolan wasn't certain what make the vehicle was. The hood had been replaced with a part from a different model that didn't quite fit and overlapped at the grille. The fender had been replaced with a makeshift wooden version. The paint was worn and chipped. Bolan wondered what jerry-built alterations had been made under the hood.

The cabbie took his time finding the Martaban Hotel. He asked his passenger how long he would be in Rangoon and if he was a stranger to the city. The driver said he knew places where Bolan could get a woman for a reasonable price, inexpensive ivory carvings, European liquor and just about anything else he might want. Bolan said he would think about it and told the guy he didn't need a tour of Rangoon at the moment. If the driver didn't know the way to the hotel, the American would get out and find somebody who did.

The driver didn't chat much after that, but he did locate the Martaban. Bolan paid the guy and included a generous tip. It was unlikely he would need to use the cabbie as a source while in Myanmar, but it was better to keep that option available, just in case.

Bolan entered the hotel and checked into his room. He didn't expect much, and he wasn't surprised by what he found. It was third-rate by American standards, the furniture resembling the sort of stuff one might find in a fifties movie. But it was adequate, and he didn't plan on spending much time there anyway.

Someone rapped against the door. The warrior wished he had a decent weapon. All he carried was a Choate "Executive Letter Opener" in his boot. Basically a plastic knife, the Choate opener was the only thing he could risk taking through metal detectors at the airports. Bolan drew the opener and held it low, by the back of his thigh.

"Who is it?" he asked.

"I have a package for you, Mr. Belasko."

Bolan carefully opened the door. A young Burmese man stood in the hall. His dark eyes looked up at Bolan, his expression calm and emotions hidden. The Executioner opened the door wide enough for the man to enter. The stranger carried a box, wrapped in brown paper, under his arm. Bolan kept the plastic knife hidden as he closed the door.

"I am Byu Lone," the man announced. "I have something for you which arrived at the U.S. Embassy in Bangkok."

"The desk clerk let you up?" Bolan asked.

"No," Lone replied. "It is very easy to get in this hotel unnoticed. There are a number of fire escapes. When we learned you would be here, we studied the place with some care. The Martaban is not that popular with foreign visitors from America or Europe. It is a good choice. Some of the other hotels have microphones hidden in the rooms by DDSI and the Special Investigations Department."

"Better figure there's a good chance they'll do that in this room after I start asking questions to the right people," Bolan said. "You said *we* studied the hotel with care. Who's with you?"

"Two fellow members of the Burma Pro-Democracy Movement," Lone replied. "I have known them for years. I would trust them with my life."

"Good. Because you're trusting them mine, too."

He opened the box, which contained a .44 Magnum Desert Eagle with shoulder holster, three spare magazines and two boxes of shells. The pistol was big and heavy, a powerful and reliable weapon the Executioner had used numerous times in the past. The other handgun was a .38 Special Smith & Wesson "hammerless" snubnose. The small 5-shot revolver wasn't a serious combat weapon, in Bolan's opinion, but it would work fine for personal self-defense as long as one didn't have to defend against a number of well-armed opponents. A belt holster, two speed-loaders and a box of shells were also included for the S&W revolver.

"Did you get the other item you required at the embassy?" Bolan asked.

"Yes. We appreciate the payment and it well help finance our resistance movement," Lone replied. "Your government is very generous."

"Okay. Let's get to business. What do you know about a Colonel Kala Thaung?"

"He's a very powerful and dangerous man, Mr. Belasko. As more authority is given to the DDSI, the more power is placed in his hands. Some of our people have seriously considered assassinating him because he has been responsible for the arrests, torture and murder of many members of the democratic movement. Thaung accuses groups like ours of being armed insurgents."

"You wanted that money to buy weapons and supplies," Bolan said. "You are getting ready for an armed revolution."

"We're training for it and arming our troops," Lone admitted, "but we don't want to carry out a bloody revolution by force. You want those guns so you can go kill people or use them to defend yourself if necessary? I practice *bando, banshay* and other martial arts. I do this for self-defense not to cause aggression. Yet, if you have to fight, you'd better know how. If there is no choice except armed revolution, you'd better be trained and equipped for it.''

"I understand. You'll try other options first."

"That's what we've been doing for the past decade. We are getting stronger and preparing for war, but we've tried to make changes by urging for free elections, civilian government and freedom of speech, assembly, a right to a fair trial, an end to torture. We had hoped major changes would occur when Win left power. I fear that it will eventually come to a violent revolt. I hope I am wrong."

Bolan nodded. He had deliberately tried to get Lone to talk about his group philosophy because he wanted a better idea of what sort of man he was dealing with. Lone seemed to be sincere, and his beliefs seemed honorable. Bolan hoped this was true and the outfit he belonged to wasn't deceiving noble young men like Byu Lone. This had happened too many times in the past.

"Okay," the Executioner began, "I've read enough about Colonel Thaung to know what you say is true. He's become our enemy as well as yours, and together we're going to put him out of business."

"What business?" Lone asked.

Bolan didn't realize the term he used was a modified form of slang. Lone's English was very good, and he forgot it wasn't the guy's native tongue.

"He's involved in heroin trafficking to the United States," Bolan said. "We're going to shut down his drug trade, end his military career, and Thaung is either going to prison or he'll be dead before I leave Myanmar.''

Lone raised his eyebrows. He had dealt with CIA in the past. They tended to be evasive and unwilling to commit to any hard action. This man was different. Whoever "Belasko" really was, he had the heart of a stalking tiger. This was a warrior, and he had already established respect from Byu Lone.

"That would make me happy," Lone said. "How do we get Thaung?"

"First, what can you tell me about the opium and heroin business in Myanmar?"

"I've never been connected with it," Lone replied. "I know most of opium poppies are grown and harvested in the Shan States. I'm familiar with the area because we've conducted training operations there. It's tropical forest and not heavily populated. However, we've had to take care to avoid the opium fields. The Meo tribesmen tend to dislike outsiders, and the ones involved with the opium will kill trespassers without hesitation. Many of the Meo are ethnic Chinese and speak Mandarin or Cantonese. They've been involved in the heroin trafficking within Myanmar. Not all of them, of course. Some of the Meo work for the Triads. Colonel Thaung isn't a Meo. It is hard to imagine the Triads would trust someone who wasn't ethnic Chinese with major drug operations.''

"I think they'd agree to it if he had an ideal method of smuggling dope in diplomatic pouches that couldn't be opened by customs and mules...carriers of the heroin, who couldn't be arrested by the police even if they got caught with the stuff on their person. If he agreed to sell the heroin directly to Triads in other countries—such as in the United States—I think that deal would sit pretty well with the in-country Triads."

"That makes sense. Thaung certainly has the political connections to accomplish that, and even members of the SLORC are afraid of him. Perhaps with good reason. Just last night a SLORC field-grade officer was assassinated. Some of Thaung's henchmen killed two college students on a rooftop and claimed they were responsible. The slain officer was known to be on poor terms with Thaung. He didn't approve of Thaung's tactics. The students were supporters of democratic reforms, but I doubt either of them would use violence. Besides, it was an odd choice that they would happen to kill an officer who was opposed to torture and oppression. One who just happened to be an enemy of Colonel Thaung."

"Sounds like more than coincidence. Gawbyan returned recently from the U.S with a cloud over his head for being involved in drug smuggling. I wonder if there could be a connection."

"It is possible," Lone said. "If Thaung has become a member of a heroin syndicate, he would almost certainly try to command the operation, and anyone who got in his way or threatened his plans would do so at the risk of his life."

"I'll bear that in mind. What about heroin use here in Myanmar? How bad is it?"

"It isn't good," Lone said. "We have an estimated sixty thousand addicts here. That's much less than in Thailand. There are ten times as many heroin addicts there, but sixty thousand is still quite a lot. A fair number of them are right here in Yangon."

"Yangon?"

"Burmese name for this city. The British somehow managed to mistranslate it into Rangoon. I believe that's what you call it."

"In what part of the city would I be most likely to find heroin dealers?"

"In the same areas where you would be most likely to get your throat cut."

"I figured that much. Where do I look?"

"There is a notorious dealer by the name of Mai Gyaw," Lone replied. "He does most of his business on Sittang Street. It isn't wise to visit that place. Especially for a white foreigner. Even a foreigner armed with a pistol as formidable as that."

He pointed to the Desert Eagle. Bolan looked at the big .44 Magnum. The Executioner would feel more confident with the familiar Desert Eagle under his arm, but he realized it was too large to conceal properly with street clothes.

"I want you to hold on to it for now," he said. "I want to disassemble it and check the parts to make sure the pistol is in good working order. After I put it back together, you take it, the magazines and the ammo with you. I'll have to make do with the .38 until circumstances allow me to pack the Eagle."

"Are you certain?"

"Too big to carry, and I don't want to leave it in the room in case the DDSI or some other security agency searches it while I'm gone."

"Very well," Lone agreed. "If you do get the attention of the authorities, I must warn you they are capable of anything. Especially Thaung. If he suspects you to be an enemy, you'll be lucky if he kills you outright. He's not squeamish about the use of torture."

"I am," Bolan replied. "Especially if I'm the one who is going to be tortured. I took on this mission with both eyes open. The last thing I'll be guilty of will be underestimating Colonel Thaung."

"If you really knew the risks," Lone said, "I'm not certain you would even be here."

11

Sittang Street proved that the view of Myanmar from the air had been false. It wasn't an exotic land of golden pagodas and lush forests. It was a country of misery, poverty and crushing despair. Rows of dwellings resembled oversize chicken coops. Thin women, dressed in rags, stood in doorways with children suffering from malnutrition.

Mack Bolan was conscious of the eyes following him as he walked through the appalling slum. The homes didn't appear to have electricity, plumbing or other conveniences most Westerners took for granted. Elderly people squatted in doorways like wrinkled gargoyles. They didn't have glasses, hearing aids, dentures or medicine for arthritis. Virtually blind and deaf, their bodies racked with pain, they seemed to be waiting hopefully for death to end their ordeal.

Bolan had considered his hotel room to be third-rate. It was a luxury suite at the Waldorf compared to the living conditions on Sittang Street. Myanmar was one of the poorest nations of Southeast Asia, and the slum reflected this. The boots Bolan wore were probably worth more money than most of these people would see in a year. He wondered what they thought of him, if they felt resentment or sorrow toward a foreigner who obviously lived a better life-style than they could ever hope to.

He searched the streets as darkness descended on the slum. There were no streetlamps, and only light from candles in the houses combated the shadows. Figures in alleys and doorways seemed more sinister in the dark. Bolan was glad he carried the .38 under his windbreaker.

Finally the Executioner located the tavern with a sign that matched the Burmese script letters Lone had written on a piece of paper. He had to use a penlight to be sure. Bolan noticed a number of unsavory characters in front of the building and in the alley beside it. Two appeared to have passed out. Others seemed to be either drunk or groggy from the effects of some kind of chemical abuse. The warrior kept an eye on them as he entered the tavern.

More drunks and addicts patronized the bar. They were slumped over makeshift tables and the counter. Prostitutes were perched on stools at the bar, their cheap makeup ghastly in the harsh yellow light cast by kerosene lamps that hung from the ceiling. As Bolan approached, one asked him in a crude language if he wanted to have sex. Her sleeveless dress revealed a series of needle track marks on her arms.

"Not tonight," the warrior said, smiling to soften the refusal.

The bartender was a round-faced man with a scrub-brush mustache. He watched Bolan as if he thought the stranger might rob the place. The Executioner placed a fifty kyat bill on the bar. The man stared at it and his eyes lighted up.

"Don't know I can change that," he said. "Don't carry too much money here. What you want, mister?"

"Gyaw. Mai Gyaw. Know where I can find him?"

"Let me get you drink," the bartender suggested. "Got some whiskey here that's not so bad. Beer is sort of flat and it's warm."

He reached for the bill as he spoke. Bolan slapped a palm on the money to pin it to the counter before the bartender could take it.

"Where is Mai Gyaw?" he demanded.

"You three days late for him," the barman replied. "How about go in the back room with one of girls? Do anything you want for right price."

"I'm not going to repeat myself. Gyaw was here three days ago?"

"I tell you where he is, I get money?"

"Yeah. That's how it works."

"Gyaw was killed three days ago," the bartender said. "Somebody stabbed him to death. He kept bad company. One of them killed him. He was cremated. Want to know where the ashes are?"

"No, thanks," Bolan replied. "Came to do business, not to honor the dead."

"He wasn't a friend of yours?"

"Never met him. Just knew his reputation. Let's be blunt. These ladies aren't alcoholics with the shakes. Where are they getting their stuff from? You?"

"Not me," the bartender replied. "They work for another man. He gives them the drugs. They just come here to do business. I get part of their money. Rent for room they use.''

The bartender grabbed the money, afraid Bolan might refuse to give him the cash after he learned Gyaw was dead. The Executioner didn't try to stop him. Instead, he placed two more fifty-kyat bills on the counter.

''Give everybody a drink who isn't already unconscious,'' he announced. ''That's about five people.''

''You still don't want drink?''

Bolan shook his head, then gestured to the prostitutes.

''Ask them about their pimp. Where does he get the drugs?''

The bartender spoke with the women in Burmese. They conversed with one another and announced they wanted twenty kyats each before they would answer the question. The barman translated the demand. Bolan put more money on the bar and the prostitutes greedily reached for the cash.

''Answer his question!'' the bartender demanded in Burmese.

''Ram Kanpur,'' a hooker stated.

''Ram Kanpur? Sounds like a Hindu name,'' Bolan said.

''He has a place called Calcutta. It is an expensive restaurant. Ram Kanpur is an Indian. There are thousands of them in Myanmar. Most don't have expensive Indian restaurants. You are rich so you can go there.''

"Thanks," Bolan said. "You people better not be lying to me or I won't be in such a generous mood when I come back."

"No lie, mister," the bartender assured him. "No reason to."

As the Executioner stepped into the street and started his trek back to the hotel, two men suddenly emerged from the alley. Dirty, painfully thin and much shorter than the American, the pair still presented a serious threat. One carried a knife with a long, rusty blade, and the other held a club with nails driven into the head. Both had eyes filled with crazy zeal.

Bolan heard footsteps behind him and glanced over a shoulder. Two more muggers materialized. He assumed they were also armed. Probably junkies, he realized. Even if he handed over all the money he carried, they would probably kill him. One of the men said something in Burmese. Bolan raised one hand as if to surrender and slowly slipped his other hand inside the windbreaker.

"Money?" he asked. "Kyat? You want money?"

Movement behind him warned of danger. The rustle of cloth and feet moving on the pavement told the warrior the guy was closing in fast. The Executioner suddenly leaped to his right as a club slashed the air near his head. Bolan dropped to one knee and drew the .38 revolver.

The knifer lunged, apparently failing to see the gun until Bolan squeezed the trigger. The report roared in the quiet, dark street, the muzzle-flash casting an orange glare across the attacking figure. Bolan saw the hole in the mugger's shirtfront leak blood as the man stumbled back from the impact of the 148-grain bullet.

The club-wielding attacker prepared to swing a stroke at Bolan's head. A leg suddenly kicked a booted foot into the man's rib cage. The mugger gasped in pain as the figure who came to Bolan's aid grabbed the mugger's wrist to wrench the club from his grasp.

The Executioner recognized his new ally. Byu Lone forced the cudgel from the mugger's fingers and smashed an elbow to the guy's skull. He yanked the stunned figure back to block the path of another attacker. The muggers collided. Lone swung a well-placed kick to a knifer's wrist to disarm him.

The two street thugs had lost their weapons, but they didn't back down. One swung a fist at Lone, who dodged the punch and parried with a palm. Lone lunged forward and slammed a knee into his attacker's abdomen. The other mugger attacked as the first tumbled to the ground, launching a kick toward Lone's groin.

A *bando* snap to the attacker's leg stomped the shin to prevent the kick from reaching the target. Lone closed in to thrust both fists into his opponent's torso. The double punch drove the mugger back, and Lone hit him with an uppercut. The guy fell to the ground, unconscious, but the first attacker was on his feet once more.

The mugger charged Lone, trying to hit him from behind. The rebel glanced over his shoulder, saw the attacker and thrust a back kick into the man's gut. Then he whirled and raised an arm high, delivering an elbow smash to the crown of his opponent's skull. The mugger dropped face first to the dirt.

Bolan rose. He glanced at the corpse of the man he had shot through the heart. The two muggers Lone had taken out wouldn't be getting up for a while, but they would survive. The fourth attacker had bolted when the gun went off. Dogs barked excitedly in the distance. No one looked out of windows or appeared at doorways. Gunshots had occurred on Sittang Street before, and residents had learned it was best not to be curious about such things.

"What are you doing here?" Bolan asked.

"I thought you might need some help," Lone replied. "This is a bad area."

The Executioner put away the .38 and both men hurried through the streets. A pair of headlights streaked through the darkness ahead. The car was moving toward them. Lone tugged at Bolan's arm and led him into an alley. They walked through the dark corridor and remained out of sight as an automobile rolled along the street. A spotlight beam shone from the car window, searching the neighborhood.

"People's Police Force," Lone whispered. "They don't generally come into this neighborhood, but they do patrol outside."

"How hard will they look for us?" Bolan asked.

"When they find the body is a common hoodlum, they won't try to find the person responsible. They would only be concerned if the dead person was a policeman, a soldier or a member of the ruling class.

Perhaps they would be upset if a foreigner was killed, because that person's government might cause problems."

"We'd better get out of here," Bolan said. "If the police ask questions in the neighborhood, somebody might mention seeing me on Sittang Street. The muggers might describe me if they're still lying around taking a nap after that beating you gave them."

"It seemed like a logical action at the time."

"I'm not complaining."

"I think you could have managed without me," Lone replied, "The People's Police Force may decide not to investigate if they discover a white foreigner was involved in the shooting. They may not wish to get into a political matter such as potential trouble with foreign embassies, and they'll turn the matter over to the Criminal Investigation Department, Special Investigation Department or even the DDSI."

"Nothing we can do about what already happened," Bolan said "Does this alley go anywhere?"

"Yes. There's a fence at the end. We can climb over it and we'll be near the road. Better not wave down a cab while we're in the area."

"I didn't intend to," the warrior assured him.

The pair climbed the fence and kept to the shadows. Another police car headed for Sittang Street. Bolan and Lone hid behind a clump of bushes until it passed their position. The Burmese rebel led the Executioner to the Shwe Dragon Pagoda. The most famous site in Rangoon and one of the most beautiful shrines in the world, the Shwe Dragon Pagoda stood one hundred yards high. Covered with gold leaf, it glittered in the moonlight.

Nine o'clock at night was an odd hour for sightseeing, but Bolan noticed some tourists at the shrine. Buddhist monks, with shaved heads and wearing robes, patiently tolerated the outsiders. Lone placed his hands together and bowed at the shrine. He lighted some incense and whispered a quiet prayer. Bolan waited for him to finish.

"Did you speak with Gyaw?" Lone asked.

"I was told he's dead. However, the bartender told me a man named Kanpur owns a place called the Calcutta. He's supposedly involved with heroin traffic. Have you heard of him?"

"I've heard of the Calcutta. Supposedly it serves the best Indian food in the city. I never heard of Kanpur, but he must enjoy a fairly good standard of living. I don't know if he makes additional income through drug trade."

"I'll try to find out tomorrow," the Executioner said. "For now, I'm going back to the hotel. I got some sleep on the plane, but I could use some more rest before going into another situation that might turn nasty."

"Be careful, and bear in mind that bartender may have given you false information about Kanpur."

"Actually a junkie said her pimp got dope from the guy. It's possible her boss lied to her for some reason or she got her information wrong."

"We'd better not leave together," Lone said. "I'll contact you tomorrow, Belasko. Sleep well."

"Yeah. By the way, Lone. Where can I buy insect killer?"

12

The Executioner sprayed the bed and blanket with insecticide, and dealt with the centipedes in the shower before using the stall. The water was cold and tinted brown.

He placed the duffel bag by the bed and put the S&W snubnose on top of it. The gun would be within easy reach in an emergency. If the authorities came for him, Bolan would be in big trouble anyway. Even if he hid the gun and the cops didn't find it, a paraffin test would prove he had fired a weapon recently. The warrior was accustomed to going to sleep with thoughts of danger and the knowledge that he was at risk.

He drifted into a shallow "combat" sleep. A sudden noise or light from the door would be enough to wake him. He wouldn't be able to enjoy a full night's sleep until the mission was over. The warrior's stomach growled slightly and reminded him he hadn't eaten for more than twelve hours.

He made it through the night without being hunted down by the police. In the morning he dressed and left the room, once again carrying the .38 at the small of his back and the speedloaders in a pocket of his jacket.

Outside, he searched for a place to eat breakfast, and had to settle for some hot tea and rice cakes at a small diner. Experience had taught him not drink water that hadn't been boiled or otherwise purified while in Southeast Asia. He also avoided milk and other dairy products. Maybe the cheese in the diner was all right to eat, but he wasn't willing to risk a case of dysentery.

Bolan killed some time at a small market, then took a cab to the Calcutta. The restaurant was the largest building of its kind he'd seen in the city. Although the roof was designed in a pagoda style, signs in front displayed pictures of the Taj Mahal and a maharaja atop an elephant. Bolan thought these looked a little odd, but he hoped he would find Ram Kanpur alive and well.

The waiters spoke English and the menu was written in three languages. The Executioner ordered meat kabobs because they were fried and steamed in their own juices, cooking out the likelihood of food poisoning. He also had curry rice and some meatballs. The food was excellent. From what he'd seen of Myanmar, good food wasn't commonplace. No wonder the Calcutta was a success.

Of course, most Burmese couldn't afford to eat in the restaurant. The customers appeared to be foreign tourists, diplomats and members of the upper class of Burmese society. A very different group of people than those he saw in the slums the night before. Bolan finished his meal and the waiter asked if he cared for dessert.

"No, thanks," Bolan replied. "But I do want to speak with Ram Kanpur. Is he here?"

"You have a complaint about the food or the service?"

"Nothing but praise for both. This concerns business. Mr. Kanpur can make quite a profit if he agrees to see me."

"I'll see if he is available."

Bolan handed the man three twenty-dollar bills and told him that was to encourage him to talk to Mr. Kanpur as soon as possible. The bribe worked. The waiter returned two minutes later and invited "Mr. Belasko" to follow him. Bolan was escorted to an office beyond the dining room.

Ram Kanpur sat behind a massive teakwood desk. He smiled at Bolan, adjusted a pair of wire-rim glasses on his nose and stood to welcome his visitor. The waiter quietly left, shutting the door for privacy.

"You wish to discuss business, Mr. Belasko?" Kanpur asked. "You are an American, correct?"

"Yeah. I'm from New York City," the Executioner replied. "A few days ago, some merchandise arrived in the city. I think a diplomat from this country delivered it. You know anything about that?"

"I own a restaurant," the Indian stated. "I am not political."

"Everybody is political. You don't have a choice anymore. I was told you might know something about the stuff in New York. Story I heard is you've been selling the same kind of stuff. Thought you might want to make a nice big sale. Like maybe four hundred kilos over a period of two years?"

"Kilos of what? Curry powder?"

"Well, I guess if you don't ship to New York I must have misunderstood and we can't do business."

"If you'd tell me what the merchandise is . . ."

"A guy named Maung Gawbyan was the diplomat. He tried to make a couple of sales to some Chinese businessmen in Manhattan. Didn't work out too well for Gawbyan. Even worse for his aides. None of this sounds familiar?"

"Not really," Kanpur replied. "It sounds like this may have been an illegal transaction. Are you asking me to break the law, Mr. Belasko?"

"No. I heard that you sold jade jewelry on the side and Gawbyan shipped the stuff in diplomatic pouches to save on postage. You like that story?"

"Are you joking, sir?"

"If you say so," Bolan replied. "Guess you don't want to know what went wrong in New York. That's okay. I'll find somebody who is interested."

"Perhaps we should talk again."

"Talk now or forget it," Bolan said. "Thanks for your time, Mr. Kanpur."

He headed out the door and passed the waiter in the corridor. The guy looked at the Executioner as if he expected to get another twenty-dollar tip. The warrior figured he had thrown around enough cash on something that might be a false lead. He shrugged at the waiter and kept going, walking out onto the street.

The warrior knew it was a long shot that he'd be able to locate a heroin dealer in less than twenty-four hours after arriving in Rangoon, or that the pusher would be directly linked to Thaung. He wasn't sure about Kanpur. The guy played dumb to a stranger, but that was expected. Of course, it was also possible that Kanpur wasn't involved in the dirty business of dope and he had no idea what Bolan was talking about.

He'd have to keep trying. If this lead didn't work, he'd find another one. Bolan had no idea where he'd find the next prospect or even where to start looking, but there was always a way if a man was determined enough.

He flagged a passing cab, climbed in and told the driver to take him to the hotel. Bolan sat in the back of the taxi and started to consider his options as to which action to take next.

A police squad car suddenly pulled away from the curb and pursued the cab, a flashing light signaling the driver to stop. Bolan felt his muscles tense as two cops emerged from the squad car and approached the taxi. One of them barked a curt sentence in Burmese. The driver gripped the steering wheel so hard his knuckles turned white. He remained rigidly fixed in his seat as one of the men opened a rear door.

"Mr. Belasko?" the policeman asked.

"Yeah. What's the problem?"

"Please, get out of the car and come with us."

"What the hell is this? Am I under arrest, or what?"

"Please, come with us. It will be better if we do not have to force you to do so."

The Executioner reluctantly obeyed. The policeman stood at attention as Bolan got out of the cab. One of them reached for a pair of handcuffs on his belt, but the warrior didn't want to be cuffed. He would be vulnerable to them, and they could frisk him and find the .38 at the small of his back.

"You put those things on me, it means I'm under arrest," Bolan said in a loud voice. "You going to do that? I demand we stop by the American Embassy. I want one of their diplomatic personnel, trained in international law, with me if you guys are going to take me in. You know, place me under arrest? Understand?"

The cops exchanged looks and said something in their own language. The officer left the cuffs in the belt case. They urged the warrior to get in the patrol car. They insisted he wasn't under arrest and someone simply wished to ask him a few questions. Bolan felt as if he were being invited to step into a lion's den with the assurance that the big cats weren't as hungry as they appeared.

However, he got into the back of the police car. At least he still had the snubnose and, if he had to shoot his way out of the situation, it would be better to wait until the car was out of the heavily populated area. There was also a chance the cops might take him straight to a police department without any detours on the way.

Both officers climbed in the front seat, a wire screen separating them from Bolan. The Executioner noticed they had not locked the back doors. That he'd managed to talk them out of using the cuffs and they had neglected the doors suggested they didn't intend to arrest him.

The squad car made its way through the streets with little trouble. There were few vehicles to compete with. People on foot and bicycles made way for the police car. The vehicle made steady progress, but it didn't head for a police station. Instead, the police drove to a canal and came to a halt by a warehouse.

The police escorted the warrior from the car and ushered him into the building. Crates were stacked along the walls. A single chair stood in the middle of the room, and two spotlights were trained on it. One policeman told Bolan to be seated. He could barely see the chair as he approached. The glare blinded him and he groped for the backrest, lowering himself into the chair.

A blurred figure appeared amid the glare. Bolan couldn't see the person's features or even estimate his height. Whoever the man was, he stayed behind the spotlights. The heat was already making the Executioner sweat, which was the idea. It was the first level of a third degree.

"Why are you asking about a shipment of merchandise sent to New York?" a voice demanded. "What exactly are you referring to, Mr. Belasko?"

Bolan raised a hand to shield his eyes. He still couldn't see the mysterious person who spoke from within the twin suns of the spotlights.

"It was a private conversation," he said. "Kanpur has a big mouth. What did he tell you?"

"We'll ask the questions and you'll answer. Kanpur thinks you were referring to drug smuggling. Is that correct?"

"I didn't say that. The U.S. Embassy isn't going to like this shit. This ain't legal."

"This isn't the United States," the voice said. "The People's Police Force brought you here for questioning. Just questioning. You're not under arrest, but you could be arrested. You're a smuggler and a drug dealer, aren't you? You can go to prison for trying to arrange to smuggle heroin out of Myanmar. This is a poor country, Belasko. Our prison system suffers from that condition. You will find our prisons less comfortable than those in your country."

"Prisons in the U.S. are such a picnic that people have trouble deciding if they want to go to Disneyland or Leavenworth."

"Is that a joke? Do you find this amusing?"

"Hardly. I figure you guys are ready to beat information out of me, and I don't even know what you think I'm supposed to tell you. Want me to say I'm a drug smuggler and I was trying to arrange a deal through Kanpur? Beat me for a couple of hours, I'll probably confess to that. Want me to say I came to Myanmar because I'm thinking about becoming a Buddhist monk? You can beat me into confessing that, too. What's your point, pal?"

"You mentioned Gawbyan. Maung Gawbyan. What do you know about him and the diplomatic pouches?"

"Kanpur must have had a tape recorder going in his office," Bolan said. "I know the same thing you know. Gawbyan was sent back here because he was accused of smuggling in heroin by using those pouches. I also know he was guilty. The American authorities couldn't touch him because he had diplomatic immunity."

"How do you know he was guilty?"

"I know what went wrong with his deals. I know why things went sour at the Chinatown gig and why his aides got killed. I know what happened to the heroin, too."

"Are you with the Drug Enforcement Administration?"

"What answer should I give so I can walk out that door?"

The voice chuckled. A long silence followed.

"I have a friend with Interpol in Hong Kong," the voice spoke. "I called him and told him to run a check on you. He'll contact the Interpol office at the United States. I believe that's with the Treasury Department or the Department of Justice. Maybe Mike Belasko isn't your real name. We'll find out."

"Great. So I have to sit here until you get a reply?"

"No," the voice replied. "We know where to find you. You're staying at the Martaban Hotel. Nothing goes on in Yangon that I don't know about. We can find you anytime we want."

"Does that mean I can go?"

"After you answer two questions," the voice said. "You claim you know why a heroin deal failed in Chinatown and how Gawbyan's aides were killed. Please explain."

"The Triad gang Gawbyan did business with was careless. They had holes in their security and another group found out about the deals. They hit 'em and got the money and the dope."

"I thought the police in New York had the heroin."

"That's what they told the news media. The people who ripped off Gawbyan's boys and the Triad took the heroin and replaced it with bags of powdered sugar. Cops don't want to admit it because it'll make them look stupid after they bragged about making a big drug bust."

"And who has the heroin? Who carried out this 'rip off'?"

"Members of the Colombian syndicate," Bolan answered. "Who else would be crazy enough to mess with the Triad in Chinatown?"

"And how do you know?"

"How else? I got connections with the Colombians. They got leaks in their security, too."

"Fascinating," the voice remarked. "We'll be in touch with you later, Mr. Belasko. Thank you for your time, and I apologize for any inconvenience this may have caused."

"Don't mention it," the Executioner replied.

He rose from the chair, careful to keep his jacket over the still-undetected .38 revolver. The police officers escorted Bolan to the door. They left the warehouse, and Colonel Thaung switched off the spotlights.

13

"A man named George Wong called," Captain Lat said. "He claimed to be with Interpol in Hong Kong. Said you wanted some information on a man named Mike Belasko."

Colonel Thaung had just returned to DDSI headquarters after his meeting with the American. The colonel gestured for Lat to follow him into his office. He didn't want anyone outside his personal circle of coconspirators to hear their conversation. Inside the room, Thaung told the captain to give him the message from Wong.

"This Belasko is an American. According to Wong's sources, he belongs to the Italian Mafia, or at least he's connected to it. Wong said Belasko served two years in prison for attempted manslaughter. He has been arrested since then, but no convictions. Interpol believes the man is a go-between with South American cocaine gangsters in Colombia or Bolivia. The DEA had him up on charges, but witnesses suddenly changed their testimony and Belasko had to be released."

"So that's who our Mr. Belasko is," Thaung said. "That's good. It explains everything."

Thaung slumped into the big leather chair behind his desk. Lat was confused and placed the report on the colonel's desktop. He handed it to the captain.

"Shred it. Destroy it, and if anyone asks, you never heard of Mike Belasko."

"Yes, Colonel," Lat replied. "Is this man important?"

"He may be our salvation, Captain," Thaung said. "I spoke with Lieutenant Po concerning how we need to establish a pipeline to America. After what happened with Gawbyan, that seemed hopeless. This could change our situation. Belasko could be our new connection to the biggest market for drugs in the world. The United States of America."

"The New York Triad won't like that," Lat said. "You made an agreement with them for direct sales. This isn't keeping with those terms."

"The Triad also assured me of security and they failed. They cost us two large shipments of heroin. Millions were lost because of their carelessness. After talking to Belasko, I know what happened. Those damn Chinese have become so arrogant they think everyone else is stupid. That's how people make mistakes. They think they're too damn clever and that makes them careless."

"That may be," Lat conceded, "but you said the Triad wouldn't be a good enemy to have."

"That's true. I also suspect the Mafia families would be very good friends to have in America. The Mafia has more power there than the Triads anyway. Everyone knows that."

"That is what they show in American movies. I'm not certain that is necessarily true, Colonel."

"Italians are Caucasian, and most Americans are Caucasian. It makes sense the Mafia could operate better in the United States than the Chinese Triads."

"All right." Lat didn't want to argue. "How do we arrange to do business with Belasko?"

"He told Kanpur he wanted four hundred kilos over a two-year period. We set a price and we agree on a general time, say a month that will be chosen with a precise date to be decided when we have another one of our people at an embassy or delegation, and start sending the shipments out in diplomatic pouches. There was nothing wrong with the method we used to send the drugs. The problem was with the Triad."

"Hopefully the American will agree to that. I don't trust Americans. They come from a completely different world than we Burmese."

"Not that different. All people are motivated by the same things—desire, love, greed, resentment, revenge and fear. Bear that in mind and you understand people regardless of their nationality."

"I still think we should be careful with this American. Belasko could be DEA or CIA."

"There's no need to worry," Thaung said. "If the American doesn't seem trustworthy for whatever reason, we'll simply kill him."

MACK BOLAN STOOD in the doorway of his hotel room and surveyed the interior. The contents of his duffel bag had been dumped on the floor and scattered across the room. The mattress was turned over on the floor. His briefcase was open, the locks broken. Stacks of twenty-dollar bills and Burmese currency were still in the valise, but Bolan noticed that some of the money was missing.

The fact that any of the money remained proved that burglars weren't responsible. The police, the DDSI or one of the other security outfits had tossed the room. They searched his stuff and didn't care if he knew it. Maybe they wanted him to know. Bolan entered the room, moved to the window, pushed back the curtain and looked down onto the street. A gray hardtop was parked along the curb. A man leaned against the automobile and stared up at the Executioner.

"Hello to you, too," Bolan muttered.

He dropped the curtain back into place. Things were happening more or less the way he expected. They had probably checked Mike Belasko through Interpol as the interrogator claimed. That was fine with Bolan. Thanks to Kurtzman's computer skills, Belasko had been a Mafia liaison for a Colombian syndicate involved with cocaine trafficking. DEA had brought charges against him, but they were dropped because witnesses backed off and the guy was running loose.

Someone knocked gently on the door. Bolan guessed who it was. The authorities would have been pounding on it—if they even bothered to knock. He turned on a small radio and raised the volume before he opened the door. Byu Lone entered.

"You know you're being watched?" he asked, then took in the condition of the room. It was obvious Bolan was aware the authorities had taken a special interest in him.

"I see you do."

"Speak softly," Bolan said. "They might have the place bugged. Are you sure they didn't see you?"

"I've been dodging these people for years. I spotted those characters outside half a kilometer away. One of them is a sergeant in the DDSI named Gyi. He's one of Thaung's men."

"Doesn't surprise me. I think I might have met the colonel."

Bolan told Lone about the interrogation and the Burmese rebel appeared startled by the story.

"You were lucky he only asked questions with a hot light in your face instead of taking you to a torture chamber."

"He wasn't going to do that. Thaung must figure I'm either what my cover makes me out to be—a Mafia soldier with Colombian connections—or I'm an agent from DEA or CIA. Either way, he wasn't going to torture me. Thaung wouldn't want to anger the U.S. government by using brutality on an American agent, and if he figured I was involved with drugs, he'll be interested in the story I told him."

"The chance to sell four hundred kilos of heroin?"

"That and the tale about the Colombians ripping off the Triad and killing Gawbyan's men. The idea that a criminal gang ruined his operation will appeal to him more than the truth. I also figure Thaung is essentially a crooked and greedy cop. He'll naturally assume all other cops are cut from the same cloth. The lie about the police covering up about the heroin is the sort of thing he'll believe."

"You're probably right. How do you manage to think the way Thaung does?"

"I've come across his kind before. There are certain variations in their personalities, but they basically think the same way. The best way to get them to believe a story is to tell them something that isn't only feasible, but also fits their notions about what the world is like."

"To be honest," Lone began, "I had doubts that there was anything constructive an American could do here, but I see now you are the right man for this job."

"Thanks. But Thaung is no fool. If he gets suspicious of me for any reason, I'm as good as dead."

"What do we do now?"

"The next move is up to Thaung," Bolan replied. "We just have to wait. The colonel will come for me, one way or the other. You and your friends will have to keep a very low profile and keep watch from a distance. If things go wrong, you might be able to bail me out."

"We'll do our best. What will you do when Thaung contacts you?"

"Pretty much play it by ear. I want him to show me the poppy fields. I want to know as much about his organization as possible so we can make sure it's destroyed completely."

"As you already noticed, Thaung has influence with the People's Police Force. He also has connections with the Special Investigations Department and probably the People's Defense Forces. That's what they call the regular army here. In short, he has eyes and ears everywhere. Don't trust anyone out there."

"I don't intend to," Bolan assured him.

The rapping of knuckles on the door startled both men. Lone pulled up his shirt to reach for a compact Walther PPK. Bolan pointed at the bathroom. The rebel nodded and moved to the other room. He stepped into the shower stall and waited. With Lone hidden the Executioner took a deep breath and moved to the door.

"Mr. Belasko?" a voice called.

"Just a moment."

The security forces surrounding the hotel might have spotted Lone sneaking into the building or seen him entering Bolan's room. It was possible they recognized the rebel. There was no way the Executioner could explain Lone.

Bolan opened the door. A man in a red jacket and bow tie looked up at him. He smiled and gestured at the suitcase by his feet. The Executioner recognized the bag.

"The airport sent me, sir," the man declared. "Your luggage finally arrived from Istanbul. Here it is."

Bolan wondered if his expression revealed his relief. He thanked the man, gave him a tip and took the bag inside. Lone emerged from the bathroom. He sighed and put the pistol away.

"One more bag for the cops to check out," Bolan said. "You'd better go, Lone."

"We'll try to keep track of what happens in case you need help," Lone assured him.

The rebel left the room. Bolan wished he could have more confidence in Lone and his group. They hadn't known he'd been grabbed by the police earlier, so how well they could keep tabs on him was doubtful. The Executioner couldn't rely on anyone but himself. Business as usual, he thought.

TWO HOURS LATER, Bolan received more visitors. He answered the door and found two men in the hallway. Lieutenant Po and Sergeant Gyi introduced themselves. They wore civilian clothing, but holstered pistols were visible in cross-draw positions on belts. Gyi was physically the opposite of Po. Short and stocky, the NCO was a stark contrast to the lanky young officer. Gyi didn't speak English and remained silent while Po spoke.

"Will you please come with us, Mr. Belasko?

"Okay," Bolan answered. "If you have your boys go through my stuff again, ask them not to make such a mess and not tear up clothes or break the locks on the luggage. I'll leave the suitcases unlocked so they can search them if they want."

"No need," Po replied. "We had that done when the luggage arrived at the airport."

"That's nice," Bolan said. "I wonder how much they stole when they did that. Some of your guys helped themselves to some of the money I had here."

"You should have put it in a secure place."

"Like this hotel has a vault?" Bolan scoffed. "You know, this money isn't mine. It belongs to the people I work for. They're going to want to know what happened to that cash."

"Tell them the truth. You lost it due to your own carelessness."

"Thanks, buddy. I'll take this up with the head man. I hope that's not you."

"No," Po replied. "You'll meet him. We're all going to have dinner together. Doesn't that sound pleasant?"

"Yeah. Wonderful. Let's go."

The Executioner followed the two men. They left the hotel and entered the gray hardtop Bolan had noticed from the window. The sergeant drove while Bolan sat in the back seat with Po. Twilight drifted across the streets of Rangoon as the car made its way through the city.

"How do you like Myanmar so far?" the lieutenant asked.

"I'm here on business," Bolan replied. "I'll do it and get out. You guys can do what you want with your own country."

Rangoon seemed gloomy after dark. There were few streetlights, and most people didn't venture outside at night. Aside from an occasional taxicab or bus, every vehicle on the streets appeared to be a police, a military or a government car. They reminded Bolan of sharks patrolling the waters of their feeding territory.

He had been in police states before. The Executioner despised such governments regardless of what label they used. Right-wing, left-wing, Communist, fascist, military dictatorship or any other variation were equally disgusting. Their tactics were similar. Perhaps even worse than the brutality employed by such governments was the fact that each tried to crush the spirit of its people. Individuality, free thought and hope were beaten down by repressive rule.

The two men with Bolan were members of such a police state. They were oppressors who preyed on their fellow countrymen. This was enough reason for the Executioner to abhor them. They were also part of the organization that shipped heroin to the United States. That made them even more culpable, in Bolan's opinion.

The warrior couldn't destroy the dictatorship in Myanmar, but he was determined to put an end to Thaung's heroin conspiracy. Po and Gyi would go down with their boss.

The car arrived at a white brick house with a tall fence. Uniformed figures armed with automatic rifles guarded the property. The gates stood open, and sentries glanced at the windshield as the car approached. They recognized Sergeant Gyi and let the vehicle pass.

Two guards waited for the men to get out of the vehicle. They were suspicious of Bolan and wanted to frisk him. Po snapped a curt sentence in Burmese and the security men backed away. Bolan followed Po and Gyi to the entrance of the house. Another sentry opened the door and saluted as they approached.

The Executioner heard shouted battle cries. Referred to as *kiai* by the Japanese, it was a universal part of martial arts practices anywhere in the world. Bolan discovered the source as soon as he entered the house. Two young soldiers were practicing kick-boxing in the hall. Stripped to the waist, they were barefoot and wore boxing gloves. The combatants dodged or blocked some attacks, but other blows landed with enough force to draw blood and produce bruises.

A harsh order in Burmese suddenly stopped the contest. The fighters stood rigidly at attention as an athletic figure appeared from the next room. Bolan recognized the face of Colonel Kala Thaung, but the photographs hadn't conveyed the catlike grace or commanding presence of the DDSI officer. Dressed in a military uniform with ribbons and rank, Thaung was the living image of a commander.

"Hello, Mr. Belasko," Thaung said. "We meet again under more pleasant circumstances."

"I recognize the voice," Bolan replied.

"Regrettable, but necessary. No spotlights will be used tonight. We haven't been introduced. I am Colonel Thaung and I am with the Directorate of Defense Services Intelligence."

He looked at the two kick-boxers. Both men were sweating and breathing hard. Blood trickled from their nostrils and mouths. Thaung seemed annoyed with the pair as he unbuttoned his jacket.

"A very poor display of our martial arts. Allow me to give you a better idea of how kick-boxing should be done."

He handed the jacket to Lieutenant Po. Suddenly Thaung leaped forward and thrust a side-kick to the abdomen of the closer boxer. The man gasped and doubled up from the unexpected blow. The second boxer threw a roundhouse kick at Thaung. The colonel's hands flashed and grabbed his opponent's ankle and pant leg.

Thaung raised the captured leg and swung a kick to the boxer's unprotected groin. The man uttered a choked moan and Thaung twisted the guy's ankle to throw him off balance. The second man fell to the hard stone floor as the first boxer recovered from the boot to his gut and attacked.

He swung a right cross to Thaung's jaw. The boxing glove cushioned the blow a bit, but Thaung's head jerked from the punch. The officer moved with his head and whirled. He extended an arm and whipped a backfist to the boxer's face. Thaung didn't wear gloves, and his bare knuckles struck hard. The boxer staggered from the blow, and the colonel snap-kicked him in the belly.

Thaung lunged forward and grabbed the man's head with both hands. He snapped his own skull forward and butted him in his already bloodied nose. Thaung held on to the dazed fighter and pumped three knee-kicks to the man's abdomen and ribs. He then shoved his opponent aside and watched him drop to the floor. The man's nose was mashed and smeared with crimson. He hugged his torso and coughed up a glob of blood.

The second boxer got to his feet. He moved awkwardly, genitals still aching from the colonel's kick. The man placed his hands together and bowed to Thaung, clearly admitting the contest was over and Thaung was the winner. The colonel responded with a high kick that slammed a shoe heel under the boxer's jaw. The unlucky trooper crashed to the floor in an unconscious heap.

"That should give them something to think about, and perhaps they'll learn from it and improve their fighting skills," Thaung announced. "Of course, they're from the Sagaing and that area isn't noted for great boxers. The best have always come from the Karen State."

"Would that be where you're from, Colonel?" Bolan asked.

"Yes, but I don't wish to boast."

Thaung retrieved his jacket and slipped into it. The Executioner glanced at the two beaten men. He felt sorry for them. Thaung had busted them up just to make an impression on his visitor. Bolan had to admit the colonel was skilled in martial arts, but the demonstration hadn't made a favorable impression on the American warrior. The two boxers were already tired and bleeding before Thaung attacked them without warning. He also had the advantage of bare knuckles and hard shoes to make his blows more effective. Besides, the soldiers would probably be reluctant to strike with full force at a commanding officer.

Still, even with these things in Thaung's favor, it had been two against one and the colonel wasn't even breathing hard. Bolan made a mental note to remember Thaung wouldn't be an easy opponent in hand-to-hand combat.

The colonel smiled at his guest. "Now," he said, "let's have dinner."

14

The dining room was spacious, and they sat at a long banquet table. The meal was Indian food. Bolan suspected Thaung had borrowed some cooks from the Calcutta. It was unlikely Kanpur would argue if the colonel wanted some of his people for a dinner party.

Captain Lat was also present. Thaung's executive officer didn't speak much and seemed suspicious of the American. Bolan assumed they all had doubts about him. Surrounded by Thaung's inner circle of trusted henchmen and armed security guards, the Executioner felt like a mongoose who had been invited to have dinner with a nest of cobras.

"You call that kick-boxing *bando,* right?" Bolan asked.

"No," Thaung replied. "*Bando* is a different style entirely. My martial art is *lethwei,* the most effective and powerful form of kick-boxing. It is superior to the Thai styles as well. Now, boxing in your country is truly amusing. They aren't allowed to kick, butt, use their elbows or knees or throw the opponent off balance. Since they wear gloves, I don't see how Western boxers ever get hurt."

"Some of them manage," Bolan said. "Actually the reason they have those rules is to try to minimize the possibility of boxers getting hurt. That's just the way Americans are. Tend to be kind of softhearted."

"Does that apply to you, Mr. Belasko?" Lieutenant Po asked. "Are you softhearted?"

"I just do what I'm told to, and I don't think much about how it affects people I don't know anyway. If people are dumb enough to use stuff that will screw up their lives, that's not my fault."

"And you're smart enough to sell it to them?" Thaung asked. "We can speak bluntly now. We are discussing heroin, Mr. Belasko. I told you I was doing an Interpol check on you. Very interesting. You used to do business with the Colombians. Now, you see the advantage of making a profit on America's rediscovered romance with heroin."

"Cocaine is still more popular," Bolan said, "but you can charge more for heroin. Besides, people are starting to snort it like coke, and some figure they can't get addicted if they just smoke or snort instead of shooting up."

"Addicts generally smoke brown heroin," Po said. "Easy to make. Just add caffeine and some other ingredients. Our chemists can manage some brown heroin if you like."

"No, thanks," Bolan replied. "We'll tap into the Chinese White market, as they call it, 'cause there's more money. By the way, you might consider procaine instead of caffeine for your brown. Dumb bastards in DEA tend to think procaine means it must be

Mexican brown. Why advertise what part of the world the stuff came from?"

"A good point," Thaung agreed. "I like doing business with men who know the trade. I am curious how you knew to contact Ram Kanpur. He's regarded as a very respectable businessman and one of the most successful Indians in Myanmar."

"I did try to get in touch with another dealer, but I found out he was dead. A little money got some junkies to cough up Kanpur's name."

"The dead dealer was named Mai Gyaw?" Thaung inquired. "He was actually too well-known and was a liability. Besides, he only wanted to do business with the Meo. Had more faith in them."

"The ethnic Chinese that live in the Shan State?" Bolan asked.

"Right again," the colonel replied. "The Meo and the Chiu Chao have been running the opium and heroin business in Southeast Asia for centuries. I say it's time the Burmese made the big profits with drugs produced here in Myanmar."

"Especially if you're one of the Burmese making the profits."

"Of course," Thaung admitted. "My power and influence here has steadily increased since the revolution. With the wealth from the heroin sales, I can buy politicians and diplomats like Maung Gawbyan. The DDSI really runs this country. The State Law and Order Restoration Council relies on us as their enforcement arm. They're handing me more power almost daily. Begging me to take it."

"I notice you got some cops on your side, too."

"The People's Police Force? Yes, Mr. Belasko. I also have followers in the People's Defense Forces and Special Investigations. More and more of them are loyal to me. Eventually this entire country will fall into our hands. You are looking at the future president and supreme-council rulers of Myanmar."

Bolan wasn't surprised the colonel planned to conquer the country and take over. A man with ambitions and lots of power wanted nothing except more power. Thaung didn't appear to be saddled with any morals or principles that might hold back his ambitions.

"That'll be nice if you can pull it off," the Executioner said. "Frankly I'm just concerned with the horse... the heroin. When can you start making deliveries to New York?"

"Next month. Possibly two months, but I'm almost certain we'll have a man in place at the delegation next month."

"Take two months if you need to," Bolan said. "Okay. How much can you ship in one of those diplomatic pouches?"

"Ninety kilos."

"Fifty is big enough," Bolan assured him. "That was one of the problems you had in New York. Big shipments are more likely to get noticed. You'll get paid. Let's just do this deal smart instead of fast."

"Agreed. Now, you want four hundred kilos within two years?"

"Maybe more if it's still movin' good on the streets. We'll let you know after the first three shipments.

Four hundred is a minimum. We'll definitely go for that much.''

"Fine. Now, let us discuss the price. The price for four hundred kilos of heroin will be twelve million dollars. I won't haggle on the price, Mr. Belasko. Twelve million."

The Executioner was surprised by Thaung's demand. The guy was serious. He really thought twelve million was a good price for an enormous amount of heroin that would net the New York dealers profits hundreds of times greater than what the colonel wanted.

No wonder the Triad had agreed to let Thaung go into the heroin business. The colonel had no idea how valuable the white powder really was. Despite his intelligence and cunning, Thaung knew only his own country. The DDSI officer thought the whole world was just like Myanmar. The Triad had been playing these guys for suckers. Thaung didn't realize people in the United States didn't live on little more than two hundred dollars a year.

"Okay," Bolan said. "Twelve million it is. We were kind of hoping for ten, but we'll do it for twelve."

The Burmese beamed, delighted with the deal.

"What about the Colombians?" Thaung asked. "Are you certain they won't steal the money and heroin this time?"

"I can guarantee that won't happen," Bolan said honestly.

"Sounds like we have a deal."

"Almost. If my people come up with twelve million dollars, they want to know for sure you can supply the heroin. Four hundred kilos is a hell of a lot of dope.''

"We can handle that amount and much more," Po stated. "Certainly you are aware that we sent almost two hundred kilos to New York before."

"Look, Lieutenant," Bolan began, "you say you can deliver four hundred kilos. I believe you, but this isn't up to me. I don't have twelve million dollars. The people who will spend that cash want proof you guys can deliver."

"We have opium poppy fields in Shan State," Colonel Thaung said. "Chemists work at the site, and we produce the heroin all in one massive operation. Since we have our own crops, we have virtually limitless supplies. Security is no problem. The DDSI has antiopium duties. Guess who is in charge of it?"

"No kidding?" Bolan asked. "Let me guess how this works. You command the DDSI officers that coordinate the regular army or the People's Defense Forces that patrol Shan State for signs of poppy fields. Of course, these are all your people. They report back that there are no poppy fields and the government figures you're doing a great job."

"Exactly. If you'd care to stay in Myanmar, I would welcome you into my organization, Mr. Belasko. You have a quick mind and you understand how these things work."

"Thanks, but I think I'm better suited to working out of New York. If you could show me the poppy fields, I think we'll have a deal, Colonel. I can report back to my bosses and that ought to assure them you can deliver."

"Excellent. I'll arrange to have my work schedule changed and conjure up a reason why I'll have to make a trip to Shan State. Shouldn't be too difficult. I'll claim there's rebel activity in the area. We should be able to leave the day after tomorrow."

"Sounds great," Bolan replied. "Meantime, could you have your people let up on bothering me? They've already searched my stuff, and somebody helped themselves to twenty thousand dollars out of my stash."

"You know about this, Lieutenant?" Thaung asked.

Po seemed uncomfortable. "Mr. Belasko mentioned it before."

"Find out who took his money. No one was told to rob from Mr. Belasko. By tomorrow afternoon you will either have his money and return it to him, or you and Sergeant Gyi will compensate him with cash taken from your own savings. Fifteen thousand from you and five thousand from the sergeant."

"I have to pay three times as much as Gyi?"

"You were the officer in charge, Lieutenant. That means you had the greatest responsibility."

"Yes, Colonel."

They finished the meal, and a box of Dutch cigars was brought out. Lieutenant Po and Sergeant Gyi excused themselves. They didn't care to socialize with the American any more than necessary, especially since he might cost them twenty thousand dollars of their own money. Captain Lat also decided to leave the table and check on the men outside.

Bolan was alone with Colonel Thaung at the table. The officer poured them each a glass of brandy. The Executioner thanked him. Thaung fired up a lighter for the cigars. The Dutch tobacco was moist and the smoke was mild. The brandy was also good quality, forming a warm sensation in Bolan's belly.

"I don't indulge in these luxuries often," Thaung said. "Too much alcohol or tobacco is no good for a man. However, this is a special occasion."

"Yeah," Bolan said. "You don't make a multi-million-dollar deal every day."

"Are you married, Mr. Belasko?"

"No. Marriage doesn't go with this line of work."

Thaung blew some smoke at the ceiling and gazed down at the brandy in his balloon glass. His expression seemed sad as he spoke.

"No, it doesn't. I was married once. My wife and son were killed some years ago."

"I'm sorry, Colonel."

"Things were different then. I was different. I even believed democracy could work in Burma until that happened. My wife and child were killed in a battle between the military and the rebels. The socialist military rule of the past and the pro-democracy forces that would be our future. This regime suits me because it isn't part of either."

Bolan didn't comment. Thaung felt like talking, so he would listen. The colonel leaned back in his chair and drew on the cigar. He blew smoke through his nostrils and tapped the ash into a glass tray.

"You have a democracy in the United States?"

"That's what they call it," Bolan replied. "People with money have a better deal than those who don't. They can afford better lawyers, tax shelters, write stuff off as business expenses and have their rich friends bail them out of trouble. Little guys get screwed. That's why I try not to be a little guy and the hell with the rules."

Thaung nodded. He liked Bolan's description of America. The Executioner had given him a version that would fit the attitude of a Mafia soldier. There was a certain amount of truth to it, but Bolan wasn't as cynical as the remarks suggested.

"I knew it was just another lie," Thaung said. "The pro-democracy people here are such fools. They think things would change for the better. They don't realize it is just another system of government that puts some in charge and others beneath them."

"How will you run the country when you take over?"

"I'll do a much better job than what's being done now," Thaung declared. "I'll continue the heroin sales until we have enough money to distribute to all our citizens. They'll be able to buy new equipment for their farms, improve businesses and start new ones. Then we'll be able to increase exports and have more and better goods. The opium fields will be used to produce morphine for medical use and the operation will be completely legal while still making a profit."

"And everybody will be happy."

"You can never make everyone happy," Thaung said. "We'll still have some enemies, but I know how to deal with them. I've been taking care of the enemies of the current government for the past three or four years. Most people will be pleased with the changes. They'll have more than they ever did before. They won't be hungry, they'll have decent homes and their children will be cared for and have new opportunities to look forward to. That's all most people really want."

"Maybe so, Colonel," Bolan replied. "Sometimes I'm not even sure what I really want."

"One goal at a time. I've enjoyed our chat, Mr. Belasko. We'll show you the opium fields and seal our deal. Then you can go back to New York and make the other arrangements. Hopefully you'll come back to Myanmar after we've established our new business line with your people."

"We'll see," the Executioner said. "My business here isn't over yet, Colonel."

15

Bolan was returned to the hotel shortly after midnight. Lieutenant Po barely said a word to him on the drive back. The junior officer was still upset about the possibility of having to cough up fifteen grand from his own piggy bank. The Executioner wasn't terribly concerned with Po. He had established a good relationship with Colonel Thaung, and the DDSI commander planned to take him to the poppy fields to see the entire operation.

The mission was going well. If everything worked out, he'd know the location of the heart of Thaung's heroin supply. How he could best deal with the situation after he got the intel would depend on whether the fields could be detected by cameras of DEA planes or spy satellites. Stony Man could bring the National Security Agency into the investigation and use their fancy SIGINT satellites to document the fields.

The government of Myanmar could be informed and left to handle the situation with Uncle Sam looking over their collective shoulder to make sure they destroyed the opium base and took care of Colonel Thaung. Myanmar wouldn't like being told what to do, but after the embarrassment with their delegation in New York, they wouldn't want to do anything that could further jeopardize relations with the United States or the Western nations in general.

Another option was to take out the fields personally. The Executioner could enlist the aid of Byu Lone and the rebels to hit the site. They could burn the crops, destroy the chemists' production center and possibly take out Thaung as well. The man was well protected, but there was always a way to get to someone.

Bolan had seen the more human side of Thaung that night. Them man was a complex collection of ambitions, sadism, grief and he had an odd paradoxical desire to be loved by his countrymen as some sort of generous uncle figure in the future. Thaung's mixed emotions combined to create a very determined character, driven by sorrow as well as greed and a lust for power, yet also convinced that the end would justify whatever methods he used.

The Executioner had no doubts about Colonel Thaung. He was a drug dealer, a torturer and a murderer. He probably didn't know how many victims he had claimed. The number was certainly in the hundreds. If he wasn't stopped, the tally would continue to rise. Bolan intended to stop him cold.

The warrior went to bed and slept better than he had the first night in Myanmar. He awoke, took another shower and dressed, about to once again search for a place that served a decent meal. A knock at the door interrupted his thoughts. Bolan hid the .38 under a blanket and answered the door. Lieutenant Po stood in the hallway. He didn't wear a happy expression.

"I have your money, Mr. Belasko. The People's Police officers sent to search your room yesterday took that twenty thousand. The idiots thought you had so much money you wouldn't miss it."

"Nobody ever has so much money not to give a damn what happens to twenty grand," Bolan replied.

The lieutenant opened a valise and extracted stacks of bills from it. Bolan noticed a lot of the money was in Burmese kyat instead of American dollars. He commented that nearly all the cash lifted from the room had been in U.S. currency.

"The three policemen who stole your money spent almost five thousand dollars last night," Po explained. "Wasted money having a party with expensive food, drink and prostitutes. One of them bought a car, but most of my savings are in kyat and British pound notes, not American dollars."

"What the hell," Bolan said. "You got most of it back and it wasn't your fault the cops had a bash with the rest."

He handed Po the bulk of the Burmese money. The lieutenant hesitated, but he took the kyat.

"You won't mention this to Colonel Thaung?"

"None of his business," Bolan replied. "This is between you and me, Lieutenant. As far as I'm concerned, you did what he told you and I got my money back. It's okay with me."

"Thank you," Po said. "I appreciate this."

The young officer was obviously pleased, and his opinion of the American improved dramatically. That was the idea. People tended to be less suspicious of someone who treated them with consideration and generosity. Besides, Bolan didn't really care about the money, but it would have been out of character for "Mike Belasko" to dismiss twenty thousand dollars without complaint.

Bolan opened the door for Po. Two figures approached as the lieutenant left. One figure was especially striking. It belonged to a young woman. Her lovely curves were displayed in a green strapless dress. The low neckline hugged her ample bust, and the hemline was higher than mid-thigh. High heels sounded on the wooden floor with the motion of her long, shapely legs.

Po didn't even look at the man with her, his attention fixed on the female as he headed down the corridor. Bolan didn't look at the woman's companion at first, either, and he didn't recognize Byu Lone until he took a better look. The rebel wore a baggy sports coat, a wide-brimmed hat and a false mustache. A pair of dark glasses completed his disguise.

"See, Mister?" Lone announced in a singsong voice. "I got a nice girl here. Young, pretty, make you happy. You like?"

Bolan let them enter his room. The woman smiled as she closed the door. Her black hair was bound in a crown, held in place by an ornate wooden clip. Her features were lovely, her lips full and her dark almond-shaped eyes large and expressive.

"You got twenty dollar American money?" Lone asked. "You get girl for two full hour."

"Maybe the lady would like some music," Bolan suggested.

He turned on the radio loud enough to mask their whispered conversation in case some of Thaung's people or hidden mikes were listening. Lone removed the dark glasses and grinned at the American.

"That was one of Thaung's officers who left," Bolan said.

"I don't think he recognized me," Lone replied. "Too busy looking at Yuzana. She is the second prettiest member of the pro-democracy movement. The prettiest is my wife, of course." Bolan looked at Yuzana. She met his gaze with approval.

"Your wife must be incredibly beautiful if that's true," the Executioner said. "Did you manage to keep track of me last night?"

"We followed the car to Colonel Thaung's fortress home," Lone replied. "Had to keep our distance and remain hidden. We were worried about you. They could have cut your throat and we wouldn't have known until your body was found in the canal."

"I was treated like a guest of honor while I was there. Thaung was real chummy. We arranged a heroin deal and everybody was pleased. More or less. I think Thaung's captain doesn't trust me any farther than he could throw this building. Sort of broke the ice with Lieutenant Po today."

"They'd all kill their mothers for a fistful of kyat," Lone said. "Don't count on any of them trusting you very much."

"I won't," Bolan assured him. "You have people in Shan State? Thaung's taking me there tomorrow to show me his opium poppies and heroin operation."

"We'll definitely be there. We've conducted training exercises there. Like I told you before, we know the area."

"Good. Hard to say what might happen while I'm there. We'll have this operation located for sure. You want to take it down?"

"Yes," Lone answered. "Gladly. How do we do it?"

"After I go for the tour we'll meet here in Rangoon. Then we get your people and go back to the site. Burn out the crops and destroy the chemists' lab where they process the heroin."

"Thaung might not be there."

"Then we'll take him out later. He's too dangerous. He could start business all over again, and he already has enough blood on his hands. If he lives, he'll start rounding up anybody he suspects might know something about the hit. We're not going to let Thaung torture and murder more Burmese or sell dope to dealers in America."

"He might go back to his house and hide there. It is well-armed and he'll feel safe there."

"He won't be. We'll blow it up if we have to. Thaung goes down with this operation. Agreed?"

"I very much agree. Now, I'd better be going. This is a long time for a pimp to spend with a client."

He headed for the door. Yuzana didn't follow him. Bolan watched her walk to the bed. She sat on the corner of the mattress, and the dress's hemline rose even higher on her thighs. Yuzana was aware of Bolan's gaze. She slowly crossed her legs.

"Lock the door," she said seductively.

16

The car passed a row of pagodas and a tall white structure that resembled the Washington Monument. Bolan got a better look at it as the vehicle drew closer. It seemed to have been inspired by a sword blade, straight and pointed, mounted on a barrel-shaped base and flanked by statues of lions. Lieutenant Po noticed the American's interest in the structure.

"That is the Independence Monument," he explained. "It recognizes our independence from the British in 1948."

The Executioner nodded. He was less interested in the historic sites of Rangoon than the poppy fields in Shan State. Po and Sergeant Gyi had arrived at the hotel at dawn to take him to the base of their heroin operations. The car headed for the railroad station, where a train waited for them. So did Colonel Thaung. The DDSI officer stood on the platform, accompanied by several troopers.

The colonel wore a fatigue uniform with a side arm on his hip. Po and Gyi saluted their commander. He returned the gesture and nodded at Bolan. The Executioner had dressed for the occasion. Boots, loose-fitting jeans, a black T-shirt—and a windbreaker that concealed the .38 revolver holstered at the small of his back—seemed appropriate attire for the occasion.

"Good morning, Mr. Belasko," the colonel greeted. "I hope you'll enjoy a ride on the train today. The railroad system in Myanmar is better than most of our roads, so this is the best way to travel to Shan State."

"As long as we get there, Colonel."

"I explained to the SLORC that it was necessary to make this trip," Thaung said. "Reports of rebel activity in Shan State had to be looked into, and I know the area very well. Better than they could imagine."

The colonel was amused by this irony. Bolan forced a smile, but he glanced at the weapons of the soldiers to get an idea what kind of firepower he might face in a confrontation with Thaung's forces. They carried a variety of assault rifles. The Type 68—a Chinese version of the Soviet AK-47—and FN FAL rifles seemed the most popular. Other soldiers packed BA-52 submachine guns. A Burmese weapon, the BA-52 was a modified version of a World War II Italian subgun, the TZ-45.

None of them carried grenades, but Bolan was sure they had some aboard the train and at the opium base. Every soldier had a fighting knife or bayonet. The warrior also assumed they were all trained in kick-boxing or some other style of martial arts. A formidable force. And Bolan had no way of knowing how many opponents would be at the base.

He discovered that dozens of troops were on the train. The soldiers were seated in at least two cars.

Bolan seemed to be the only passenger dressed in civilian clothes, and he wondered what sort of excuse Thaung had come up with to explain the presence of a white foreigner. Whatever he told them, he doubted anyone would question Thaung's story. The colonel seemed to be able to do virtually anything he wished.

The Executioner joined Thaung, Po and Gyi in a car separated from the regular troops. Breakfast was served as the train pulled from the station. Bolan was pleasantly surprised to discover coffee was ordered as well as tea. Thaung explained that it had been imported from Indonesia. Most of the food was fruit. Fresh bananas, oranges and mangoes with boiled rice wasn't Bolan's idea of a hearty breakfast, but by Burmese standards it was a feast.

Captain Lat wasn't on board. Bolan was relieved, because Thaung's second in command seemed especially suspicious of the American. Apparently Lat had remained in Rangoon to act as temporary commander in Thaung's place. Since Lat was due to be promoted to field-grade rank, this was a valuable experience.

Bolan had a window seat and took advantage of the chance to see more of Myanmar as the train headed northeast toward Shan. The cities they passed appeared much smaller than Rangoon, and many towns looked almost primitive. People lived in huts with no evidence they had electricity, phone lines or plumbing. More examples of the terrible poverty that plagued Myanmar.

The train crossed bridges extended above rivers and canals, and Bolan noticed many small boats traveled the latter. In fact, it seemed the canals were a more important form of transportation than the railroads. Many boats were loaded with crates of merchandise en route to markets in different locales.

Hundreds of paddies lined the rivers. Farmers labored among the crops, wading in knee-deep water. They barely glanced up at the train. The paddies were their lives and fed their families. Trains weren't an important part of the farmers' world, and they had too much to do to be concerned with a machine rolling past them.

The train ride was a fairly long journey and covered more than five hundred kilometers. Colonel Thaung spent much of the trip asking Bolan questions about the United States and New York City. The Executioner answered them as he thought a Mafia wise guy would. He had impersonated mafiosi before and successfully pulled it off even when he performed the act for capos and street soldiers in the Mob. Convincing Thaung he was for real was easier. The man's concept of American organized crime came from what he'd seen in the movies.

The train came to a halt near a lumber operation outside the city limits of Mawkmai. Three trained elephants were among the workers. Handlers sat on the backs of the huge animals and urged them to lift heavy logs and wooden beams with their trunks and feet.

Bolan didn't realize they were in Shan State until Lieutenant Po mentioned it. The Executioner, Thaung, Po, Gyi and a dozen other soldiers left the train. The rest of the troops remained on the locomotive to move on to a military base somewhere in the state. Bolan, Thaung and the others walked to a pair of army trucks and three Land Rovers. More uniformed figures waited for them by the vehicles.

Sergeant Gyi slid behind the steering wheel of one Rover. The Executioner and Colonel Thaung climbed into the rig. Lieutenant Po joined an NCO in another vehicle, and the troopers loaded into the trucks. The caravan headed north, and Bolan was beginning to wonder how much longer it would take to reach the heroin center. There were no railroad tracks or roads where they were going. Other than some dirt paths worn into the ground by frequent use, there was nothing but rough earth to travel across.

Soldiers riding shotgun stayed alert, weapons held ready, as they drove through dense forest areas. Thaung explained that the troops weren't only concerned about rebels and bandits, but they were also worried that man-eating tigers might be hiding in the bush. Supposedly, years earlier, fourteen soldiers were killed by tigers in the Arakan Yomas mountain range.

AT LAST they reached their destination. Armed sentries guarded the field of opium poppies. The crops covered close to two hundred square kilometers. Figures moved within the fields, inspecting and picking poppies. Five buildings had been erected, and several trucks were parked in a motor-pool area. Gasoline tanks were positioned near the rigs, and two generators sat at different ends of the compound. Cables extended to the buildings, and lines of light bulbs were strung along posts throughout the base.

"We have arrived," Thaung said. "What do you think, Mr. Belasko? Have you ever seen anything like this before?"

"Not lately," Bolan replied.

It was quite a setup. Field laborers carried sacks full of poppies to one of the buildings. They emerged with empty bags and headed back to the fields. Soldiers stood by the entrance to another building and watched the caravan roll into the compound. Uniformed men flooded from two of the structures. Bolan tried to guess the number of soldiers stationed at the base. More than fifty. Maybe twice that number. This seemed to be a twenty-four-hour-a-day project, so some of the men were probably asleep.

Bolan and Thaung stepped from the Land Rover. The colonel waved a hand at the flowers. The poppies seemed frail and innocent, yet the corruption of man bred them and plucked them for evil purpose.

"We're going to plow out more ground and plant another field soon," Thaung said. "Our poppies grow very well because we supply them with everything they need. See those pipes?"

He pointed at a series of tubes that stretched from a huge aluminum silo to the fields of poppies.

"Irrigation," Thaung said. "Poppies grow best with plenty of water. We have a resident horticulturist here to make certain the plants are growing and healthy."

The colonel headed for the buildings, followed by Bolan. Two men with sacks hurried past him on their way to deliver more poppies.

They entered the building. More workers were busy clipping the tiny fruit from the poppies. A man with a long glass tube studied a gellike substance in a metal tray with a sun lamp positioned above it. Thaung pointed at the ooze.

"That, my friend, is opium," he said. "Simply dried sap from the poppy capsules or fruit. The chemists tell me it contains some alkaloids used for the production of such medical wonder drugs as morphine and codeine. Unfortunately for most, but quite fortunate for us, these drugs can have an addictive effect if misused."

They moved on to a large glass cubicle. Two men dressed in white smocks and wearing protective masks were inside the transparent box. They studied the contents of three vats, then carefully poured liquid into them.

"The men are producing morphine," Thaung explained. "Very simple process. A German pharmacist discovered the method in 1806. Liquid ammonia added to opium makes a white powder that can be used as a painkiller. Morphine was used during the Civil War in the United States. I believe there were even some farmers who managed to grow poppies, and America produced its own."

He escorted Bolan through the side door of the building to the next structure. More masked men labored over stoves with pots on the hot ranges. A pungent stench revealed why these chemists needed to protect their faces.

"This is more morphine being boiled with a chemical called acetic anhydride," Thaung said. "After several hours the contents will be transformed into what Western scientists call diacetylmorphine, but it is better known to most of us as heroin.''

More workers scooped out white powder from a vat and filled plastic bags. Each contained half a kilo, Bolan reckoned. Hundreds of bags were already mounted on tables. A controller kept an eye on the baggers and made certain they used the measuring scoop to get precise weight for each container.

''And here is the finished product. As you can see, it is being prepared for market.''

''Yeah,'' Bolan said. ''You've got this set up pretty good. You were serious when you said the supply was virtually limitless.''

''In fact we'll be increasing production when we can afford to expand. We also intend to sell more to other countries besides the United States. There's a good market in parts of Europe, especially Great Britain, and in Australia and New Zealand. There are approximately two hundred thousand heroin addicts in Australia. That's a very high number considering the entire population is less than seventeen million.''

''Supply and demand,'' Bolan said. ''You got the supply and they have the demand.''

''Exactly. As you can see, I'll have no trouble supplying your people in New York.''

''I can go back to New York and assure them of that,'' Bolan said. ''I'd say we might be doing business together for years, Colonel.''

''I certainly hope so,'' Thaung replied. ''Is there anything else you'd care to see?''

"No. I've seen everything I have to. Now, if you'll take me back to Rangoon I'll get the next flight back to the States."

"We'll leave at dawn. It is dangerous to travel at night in this area. It is unlikely bandits would attack us, but rebels are a serious threat."

"Don't forget the tigers."

Thaung laughed. "My men are more worried about that than I. Some are afraid to travel in the jungle because of the Kung-Tu. It's a monster they claim dwells in Shan State. Sort of like the yeti in the Himalayas, but this one is supposed to be bigger. They say Kung-Tu is seven meters tall, tears up trees and eats people."

"Sounds like King Kong with an attitude."

"Even if such a creature existed, I doubt it would be any match for automatic weapons. We don't have your Empire State Building for the Kung-Tu to plunge to his death, but I don't think that would be necessary."

"Well, I don't want to upset your men so I guess we'll spend the night here."

"You'll find the quarters are relatively comfortable," Thaung said. "We also have a Chinese cook here. I understand we have a number of pheasants in the freezer unit. I'll have him prepare them for dinner. We do have reason to celebrate tonight."

"Yeah," Bolan agreed. "I guess we do."

He didn't relish spending the night in an armed camp of his enemies. So far his cover had held fast and Thaung seemed to trust him, but the longer Bolan remained with them the more likely something could go wrong. He couldn't think of any logical reason why he should insist they go back to Rangoon immediately.

The Executioner knew the value of patience and knew everything would go well, as long as he continued to play his role. Night would pass, and they would return to Rangoon. Then he could contact Byu Lone and plan their attack.

17

The meal was prepared and ready two hours after sundown. They ate outdoors, seated on the ground with wooden bowls and plates. The pheasant was cooked Szechwan-style with a bit more red pepper than Bolan cared for, but the rice, boiled vegetables and bananas compensated for the abundance of spice. Coffee as well as tea was offered with the food.

The electric light bulbs added to the festive atmosphere. Strung above the picnic area, the lights could have been decorations at a party or an expensive restaurant that offered dining outside. Uniformed troops took turns eating and standing guard. The chemists and field workers took a break from their labors to join the celebration. Voices conversed in several languages. Colonel Thaung seemed to be the only person who understood what everyone was saying.

Some soldiers played guitar, a wood flute and a set of drums. Others sang a martial song. Bolan wasn't sure what the song was about. Burma's last major military victory was more than eight hundred years earlier when the Pagan Kingdom drove back Chinese invaders. No one was trying to conquer Myanmar, unless one included the pro-democracy forces who still hoped to change the country through peaceful methods.

Other entertainment consisted of Colonel Thaung's favorite contact sport. Troopers clashed in *lethwei* contests. The kick-boxers removed their boots, but didn't wear protective gloves. Since they were trying to please the colonel, the boxers fought hard and showed no concern for the possibility of injuring each other. Bare knuckles and feet slammed into flesh. Men fell, and their opponents kicked them until a referee called the contest off.

A *banshay* demonstration followed. This was a form of Burmese martial arts using weapons. When a guy stepped forward with a sword in each fist, Bolan figured somebody was going to get killed. However, the swordsman didn't fight. Instead he performed a sword dance. He whirled the blades close to his own body and he leaped and danced to a drumbeat. The guy displayed considerable skill. Bolan noticed Thaung was bored by the sword dance. If it wasn't bloody, it wasn't entertainment to the colonel.

Thaung's interest increased when two men squared off with staves for another demonstration of *banshay*. One contestant was large for a Burmese and heavily muscled. He smiled at his smaller opponent as they whirled the long sticks in preamble to battle.

Staves clashed as the combatants attacked and countered with the wooden weapons. The smaller man was faster and swung a stroke to the big guy's ribs. It had no effect. The brute quickly chopped his staff across his adversary's shoulder. Bone crunched and the joint disconnected. The smaller man's face was contorted in pain, and his arm dangled at his side, limp and useless. Despite the injury, the contest wasn't terminated. The little guy showed his courage and attempted to thrust the end of his stick into his opponent's solar plexus, but the man parried the attack with his own staff.

A backhand sweep slashed the pole across the smaller man's skull. The unlucky fighter dropped to the ground, blood oozing from a wound by his temple. The brute charged, raised his stave high and stamped one end in the center of the fallen man's chest. Bone cracked once more as the sternum shattered. The man on the ground twitched and lay still. The burly victor raised his stave, but only a few voices cheered.

"He got carried away in the contest," Thaung said. "It was not supposed to go this far."

"Yeah. A guy getting killed kind of puts a solemn note on a celebration."

The corpse was dragged away. Bolan noticed the big killer didn't seem upset about the incident. Only a handful of his comrades congratulated him and gathered around the cruel victor. The majority of Thaung's followers regarded the man with loathing.

"Perhaps that's enough demonstration of the fighting arts," the colonel said. "Let's see about your sleeping quarters, Mr. Belasko."

Bolan nodded. Thaung and Po headed for one of the buildings. The Executioner figured he should follow. They were going to a structure that wasn't used for heroin processing or billets for troops. Bolan assumed it was a head shed, Thaung's personal HQ while at the base. The building was large enough to have guest rooms as well as quarters for the colonel and his staff.

Before they reached the entrance, a man appeared at the threshold. He saluted and said something in Burmese. The guy seemed concerned. Thaung replied in whatever tongue they spoke and turned to Bolan.

"Captain Lat has radioed ahead to tell us he's flying here in a helicopter," Thaung said. "He claims it is important. For his sake, it better be. I ordered him to stay in Rangoon and I didn't authorize coming here in an aircraft."

"That isn't good," Bolan said. "Regular military must use radar for general security reasons. They'll have a pretty good idea where he is when he lands. Somebody is going to ask what the hell he's doing in an obscure part of Shan State in the middle of the night."

"Don't worry," Thaung urged. "We'll make certain any questions are satisfied. I can tell the SLORC and the People's Defense Forces the helicopter was called in to help us hunt for rebels by using infrared scans from the air. First, Captain Lat had better be able to convince me his trip here is necessary. The reason we didn't fly out here from Rangoon is the very one you mentioned. It isn't security-sound."

Po took Bolan inside and showed him a room as the sound of rotor blades chopping air announced the approach of the helicopter. Thaung's anger increased as he marched outside. Lat had obviously waited to inform them of his visit until the helicopter was already well into the state. He wanted to be certain Thaung didn't deny him permission to land.

The colonel stood outside and watched the lights of the chopper move slowly across the sky. The helicopter closed in and hovered over the compound, then descended to the parade field in the center of the base. Surprised troops stood by and watched. Captain Lat personally piloted the aircraft. He emerged after touchdown with his only passenger, Maung Gawbyan.

"What are you doing here?" Thaung demanded. "And why did you bring Maung?"

"Something always bothered me about Mr. Belasko," Lat said. "His story sounded good, but there seemed to be something wrong."

"Answer my question, Captain," Thaung demanded. "The fact that you don't like Mr. Belasko isn't an adequate reason for this violation of basic security."

"Please, let me explain," Lat urged. "I recalled Maung Gawbyan's description of the attackers at the Chinese restaurant in New York. All of them were dressed in odd costumes with strange hair dye and bizarre jewelry, except one man. That description of the individual Maung saw from the car sounds very much like Mr. Belasko."

"That description would fit hundreds of Occidentals."

"Let's make sure," Lat replied. "I brought Maung here to see Mr. Belasko personally. If he recognizes the American, it means the man is really an agent for the DEA, CIA or some other government agency, sent to destroy us.''

''This is absurd. Why would they send the same man here?''

''I don't know, Colonel,'' Gawbyan admitted, ''but I agree with Captain Lat. If there is any possibility, no matter how slight, that Belasko is the same man I saw in New York, we need to find out.''

''You're here now so we may as well get this over with,'' Thaung said. ''After this is finished, I'll decide what action to take. Someone is going to regret this, Captain. Either you or Mr. Belasko.''

MACK BOLAN SAT on the bunk in the guest quarters. The room was small, but relatively comfortable. The bed was in better shape than the one at the hotel, and Po had given him clean sheets, pillow and case from a linen closet. The lieutenant also handed him some bottled water, a small battery-operated radio and a roll of toilet paper with verbal directions to the latrine.

The warrior unzipped the windbreaker and slipped out of the jacket. He unclipped the holstered .38 and tucked it under the pillow. He was preparing to remove his boots when someone knocked on the door. It opened before he could ask who was there or give permission to enter. Lieutenant Po looked at him with a blank expression.

''The colonel needs to talk to you for a couple of minutes before you go to bed.''

''Okay,'' Bolan replied. ''I'll be there in a couple of seconds.''

"Now, Mr. Belasko," Po said. "He wants to see you right now."

"Just going to tie my bootlaces," Bolan said. He started to rise from bed and slipped his arm under his jacket. The Executioner kept his back to Po to block the lieutenant's view as he grabbed the revolver from beneath the pillow. Bolan draped the windbreaker over his forearm to hide the gun as he headed for the door.

"Is anything wrong?" the warrior asked.

"Let's hope not."

Bolan entered the main room. The radio operator was still at his station. Colonel Thaung stood at the end of a long table. Two soldiers accompanied the colonel, weapons held at port arms. Captain Lat was near the front entrance. Maung Gawbyan stood beside him. The diplomat's eyes widened when he saw the Executioner. Gawbyan pointed a finger at Bolan and shouted something in Burmese. The warrior didn't need a translator.

His cover had just been burned.

18

"That's him!" Gawbyan said. "That's the man!"

Thaung was startled by the announcement. He stared at Mack Bolan as if the American had suddenly transformed into a king cobra. The soldiers reacted without trepidation. They pointed their weapons at the warrior. Captain Lat reached for his side arm. Lieutenant Po was puzzled, uncertain what had happened.

The Executioner reacted swiftly. His fist appeared from beneath the windbreaker and he triggered the .38, the gun bellowing in the confines of the room. A trooper's head snapped back as a 148-grain semi-jacketed hollowpoint blasted through his skull. The report of the revolver still sounded within the four walls as Bolan swung his other fist and hammered it into the side of Po's jaw.

The lieutenant fell from the unexpected blow. Bolan dropped to one knee an instant before the second trooper opened fire. A stream of 7.62 mm slugs snarled from his assault rifle. The bullets passed above Bolan's head as he returned fire. He squeezed off two rounds rapid-fire. Both .38-caliber stingers hit the gunman in the chest, ripping through the guy's heart. The rifle slipped from the soldier's grasp as he collapsed lifeless to the floor.

Bolan saw Thaung duck for cover at the end of the table, but he realized Lat presented a more immediate threat. The captain had already drawn his weapon and was trying to aim it at the Executioner. The warrior saw Lat's legs under the table, green uniform pants clearly recognizable. The warrior aimed and fired. Lat screamed as a slug smashed into his thigh just above the knee. The captain crashed to the floor hard. His pistol was jarred from his hand and skidded across the floor.

The guy was unarmed and no longer an immediate threat. Movement at the end of the table warned that Thaung was drawing his piece. The Executioner shoved both forearms into the table and stood. The furniture suddenly flipped up and toppled onto the colonel. Thaung sprawled on the floor, pistol in his fist.

Bolan started to aim his revolver, but the radioman had scooped up the slain soldier's T-68 rifle and was already swinging the barrel toward the Executioner. Bolan swiftly adjusted the aim of his weapon and fired the last round. The radioman fell backward into his transceiver, blood spurting from the side of his neck.

The warrior was out of ammo and still faced armed opponents. Thaung and Po were dazed, but both carried pistols. Bolan couldn't jump one man without leaving himself vulnerable to the other. His only chance of survival was to flee. Since the base was crawling with troops, he realized the odds were still pretty bad regardless of what he chose to do.

There was no time to dwell on mental debates. He bolted for the door. Maung Gawbyan jumped back, terrified and unaware the gun in Bolan's hand was empty. The warrior jumped over the prone figure of Captain Lat and darted through the open doorway. A pistol cracked as the Executioner reached the threshold. A blur of motion behind Bolan caused him to glance back. Gawbyan fell against the doorway and slid through the entrance. A bullet hole under his left shoulder blade revealed where Gawbyan had stopped a slug meant for the Executioner.

Soldiers ran to the HQ, drawn by the gunshots. More than a dozen armed figures headed toward Bolan. He raised his arms and waved them in a frantic gesture. Bolan pointed at the building with one hand and pulled the trigger of the .38 with the other. The revolver clicked harmlessly as he kept the muzzle aimed at the sky to make certain none of the troops felt threatened.

"Inside!" he urged. "Get inside! Colonel Thaung needs help! Hurry, Lat went crazy! Hurry!"

That any of the soldiers understood English was hard to say, but they all understood that Bolan seemed terrified and was trying to steer them to the building where the shooting occurred. He had an empty gun so he wasn't a threat, and they had seen how Thaung treated the American like visiting royalty. The troopers moved to the head shed and ignored Bolan. Some took position outside, staying clear of the doorway, while two dived through the entrance, weapons held ready.

Bolan never stopped moving. Even as he waved the troops to the building, he was backing away at a quickstep. He heard voices shout with anger. Thaung was telling them what happened, and the soldiers would be after Bolan in less than a second. He didn't intend to make it easy for them.

The Executioner ran to a barracks and jogged around the corner, almost running into two soldiers on their way to investigate the gun battle. Bolan came to an abrupt halt and raised his arms. The troopers stopped, confused by his actions. They didn't know if he was trying to surrender or just afraid they might shoot him if he didn't show he was not a danger to them.

"Easy, guys," he said. "Here. Take it."

He reversed the grip on the revolver and handed it butt first to the closer trooper. The guy accepted the gun. Neither he nor his companion pointed his weapon at the Executioner. They were likely afraid of upsetting the visitor who was obviously Thaung's guest of honor.

Bolan suddenly grabbed the barrel of the soldier's BA-52 submachine gun with one hand and slammed his other fist into the man's face. He rammed a shoulder into the stunned trooper's chest and shoved him into the second soldier. Bolan wrenched the subgun from his opponent's grasp and drove the buttstock into the battered man's gut.

The second soldier raised his rifle, but Bolan was too close. The Executioner raised the barrel of his confiscated weapon and struck the enemy's T-68. The blow knocked the soldier's gun barrel skyward. Bolan quickly hit him with a butt stroke to the side of the skull before the guy could react. The soldier tumbled to the ground, a crimson bruise at his temple.

The first soldier recovered from the blow to his abdomen and lunged for Bolan's neck. The warrior whirled and whipped the barrel of the BA-52 across the guy's forearms to deflect the attack. He followed the counterattack with a left hook to the soldier's jaw. The guy staggered, and Bolan slashed the gun barrel across his skull. He dropped to all fours, too dazed to continue the attack.

A voice shouted something in Burmese. Bolan didn't look back as he raced toward the rear of the barracks. A burst of automatic gunfire chased the warrior. He reached the corner of the building without stopping a slug.

Bolan jogged along the wall of the building. Two armed figures appeared at the opposite end of the structure. The warrior opened fire and nailed both soldiers before they could trigger their weapons. He turned, suspecting the gunman in hot pursuit would try again. A uniformed figure poked a rifle barrel around the edge of the building and the Executioner triggered another short burst. Scarlet sprayed from the dome of the gunman's head.

Voices shouted throughout the base. Bolan knew the troopers were disoriented by the unexpected outburst, but Thaung would soon organize them and begin a systematic search. They would expect him to make a dash for the forest beyond the base and would cover exits at the perimeters of the compound. With electric lights strung across the area, it would be almost impossible for Bolan to attempt an escape.

He wasn't sure how many rounds were left in the BA-52. The weapon was unfamiliar to Bolan, but it was similar in design to others he had used. The gun was a simple blowback action, full-auto weapon. Bolan wasn't certain of the BA-52's magazine capacity, but if he had to make a guess, he'd say around a 40-round magazine capacity. Bolan guessed he had burned up roughly ten rounds, but he wasn't certain.

The warrior figured the best thing to do was what they wouldn't expect. He wouldn't try to escape. Not yet, as least. He heard boot leather shuffle at both ends of the barracks. They were aware of his position and planned to trap him in a cross fire. If he stayed put he'd be cut to pieces, and if he tried to run away they'd pick him off. Bolan noticed plants weaving violently among the poppy fields. Men were low-crawling through the crops. They were going to block off that route and possibly form a semicircle attack force.

The warrior moved to a window. It was open. He used the gun barrel to punch out the screen and climb over the sill. He slipped inside the barracks. The building was empty. Everyone was outside hunting him.

Almost everyone.

Three soldiers entered the barracks. They hadn't forgotten about the windows. Bolan dropped on his belly and slid under a bunk. He remained still as the trio approached. They hadn't noticed the missing screen in the window, but the warrior figured they'd see it after they finished glancing at wall lockers and pillar supports. He was also aware they might spot him before they got around to the windows.

Gunfire erupted outside. The troops had carried out their cross fire, apparently blazing away from both ends of the billets without bothering to see if Bolan was still there. The Executioner took advantage of the distraction and the noise to roll from beneath the bunk. He knew the troopers would see him if he tried to move. There was only one option he could take.

Bolan opened fire. He hit the closest soldier with a trio of bullets in the chest. Before the first man fell, the warrior blasted the second with another short burst. The guy was pitched backward onto a bunk and flopped across the mattress. The sheets beneath him were stained by a steady flow of red.

The third soldier jumped for a pillar and raised his T-68. A hasty salvo of 7.62 mm slugs raked the wall above Bolan's position. The Executioner's aim was true as he triggered another salvo, taking the gunman out of play. The corpse slid down the pillar to the floor.

The shooting outside continued. Bolan hoped it had masked the exchange between the three soldiers and himself. The warrior jogged to the nearest corpse and found two spare magazines for a BA-52. He removed the depleted mag from his weapon and replaced it with a fresh clip. Bolan took the magazine from the dead man's weapon, stuck the spare mags into his belt and headed for the west wing. He glanced out a window. A line of soldiers advanced to the rear of the barracks. They ventured around the corner to see if they had shot down their enemy. Boots pounded the floor as more troopers entered the billets. They immediately saw the slain bodies of their comrades.

The soldiers would also spot Bolan in another second or two. He made a snap decision and quickly acted. The Executioner grabbed the corner of a wall locker and leaped at a window. He guided his jump and dived feet first through the screen, plunging through the opening and hurtling outside. His boots slammed into the shoulder and neck of an unsuspecting trooper.

The guy went down hard, vertebrae dislocated by the impact. Bolan toppled to the ground beside the man. A startled soldier stared down at him, then lashed a boot at the warrior's subgun in an effort to disarm him. The Executioner slammed the gun barrel across the trooper's shin to block the kick. The man stumbled and hopped back on his other foot. He decided to use his gun instead of trying to take Bolan with kick-boxing tactics, and raised his rifle. Bolan shot him between the eyes.

The Executioner heard voices, and running feet heading toward his position. They were coming from all directions. Too many of them, Bolan realized. He knew he couldn't take them all. As the warrior dashed for the two buildings used for preparing morphine and heroin, he knew there was no way out. If this was to be his last battle, the warrior would go down fighting. If he couldn't destroy Thaung and his operation, at least he could hurt them.

A dozen armed figures charged after the fleeing American. Weapons roared and orange flame streaked from the muzzles of several rifles and subguns. Bolan ran backward and pointed his BA-52 at his opponents, but he held his fire when he realized none of the enemy bullets came close to him. The troops had fired into the air. They were trying to get him to surrender. Thaung must have ordered them to take him alive if possible.

Bolan kept moving, triggering his subgun and spraying the enemy with a horizontal slash of bullets. Three troopers went down as the others opened fire. Slugs tore into the earth near Bolan's running feet. They were still trying to take him alive and hoped to shoot his legs out from under him. Clods of dirt splattered his legs and a bullet ricocheted off a rock to tug at the warrior's shirt fabric.

The Executioner moved faster, knowing Thaung would interrogate him, using the skills he'd developed from years in torture chambers. The colonel would make Bolan's death as slow and painful as possible. The relatively quick end from a bullet would be merciful compared to such a horrendous ordeal.

Bolan fired his subgun as he ran and saw two more soldiers tumble from the ranks. The enemy was no longer trying to take him alive, and the next volley was directed at torso level. However, they weren't marksmen, and were unfamiliar with gun battles. The shots were poorly aimed, and bullets ripped into the wall of the building behind the Executioner.

One slug struck at Bolan's abdomen, hitting a magazine that was jammed in the warrior's belt. The impact of the bullet drove Bolan backward as if kicked in the belly. A cartridge in the mag detonated and the explosion doubled the force of the blow. Bolan was knocked off his feet and hurled into the side of the building.

The pain forced a gasp from the Executioner. He clamped a hand over the wound between his hip and rib cage. His palm jerked back when it connected with flame. His shirt had caught fire when the cartridge blew. He slapped at the material and extinguished the flame. The flesh under his charred shirt throbbed with pain as he rolled onto his knees and used his subgun to force open the door.

Bolan rolled inside and kicked the door shut. The warrior pulled the damaged magazine from his belt. The top portion was ragged and deformed from the effects of the projectile and the exploding shell. Bits of metal had punctured flesh, and the skin had been scorched by the powder burn.

He discarded the useless magazine and pointed his BA-52 at the door. No one charged through the entrance. The pulse behind Bolan's ear thundered loudly, and he wasn't certain if the enemy was still shooting at his position. He forced himself to breathe deeply. They had ceased fire, he realized. Probably reluctant to damage the building that stored poppy sap and morphine. But they wouldn't hold back for long.

Bolan groaned as he climbed to his feet and latched the door. He took the remaining, undamaged magazine from his belt and removed the depleted one from the BA-52. He shoved in the fresh mag, aware that it was the last of his ammo. From now on every round had to count.

He saw his first target and pointed the subgun at the glass cubicle used for morphine production. Bolan aimed at the large plastic bottles inside the glass cage and squeezed off a short burst. Glass shattered, and the ammonia spilled from the punctured containers. He used the gun barrel to tip over the trays of opium sap. The substance would soak up too much ammonia and become useless.

The toxic fumes from the ammonia forced the warrior to cover his nose and mouth. He rushed to the rear exit as troops broke down the front door. The ammonia hit the men without warning and they coughed and gagged from the fumes. Bolan didn't waste ammunition on them and darted outside.

A uniformed figure appeared at the rear of the building. He had expected to cover the back door, but wasn't prepared to find himself face-to-face with the Executioner. Bolan quickly pumped a trio of slugs into the guy's chest, then dashed to the next building as more soldiers materialized. Luckily the heroin processing center was very close to the morphine center, and Bolan hit the door before the troops could pick him off.

Bolan slammed the door and shoved a bolt into place. He glanced around the single large room. There were two windows, but no other door. His burned side generated a wave of pain as he moved to the stoves used to boil morphine. The warrior opened the back of a stove, a crude portable model that burned kerosene. Good, he thought. Kerosene burned hotter than gasoline.

He removed the tanks of kerosene fuel from both stoves and carried them to the stacks of bagged heroin at the opposite end of the room. He doused the contents of one tank across the dope. Pounding at the door warned that the enemy was trying to break it down. A face appeared at the window and a gun barrel smashed glass from the pane.

The Executioner dropped to the floor as the gun swung toward him. He shoved the second kerosene container to the pile of heroin. Voices shouted outside. The man at the window held his fire. They were worried about the heroin. No wonder. A spark from the muzzle-flash could ignite the kerosene and burn up all the dope. Hundreds of kilos worth millions would literally go up in smoke.

The warrior crawled away from the drugs and the aim of the gunman at the window. His side protested the movement, and half of his body felt numb with pain. Bolan tried to shut off the effects of the pain. He needed a steady hand for what would probably be the last act of his life. The Executioner would ignite the kerosene and make a final stand outside. They'd kill him for sure, but he'd try to take as many of them with him as possible.

The door suddenly burst open. A trooper charged across the threshold and dived to the floor in a roll. The trick would have worked against a less experienced man. Bolan tracked the movement and blasted a three-round burst into the tumbling form.

Another figure at the doorway pointed a pistol at Bolan. The warrior ducked as the handgun bellowed. A slug punched the wall above his bowed head as Bolan returned fire. The gunner screamed and jerked backward from the impact of the high-velocity rounds to his upper torso. Time was running out fast. Bolan swung the BA-52 toward the heroin, fixed the sights on the stone floor under the tables and squeezed the trigger.

Bullets struck stone. Sparks ignited and touched off a pool of kerosene. Flames rose swiftly, and the tables and dope were shrouded in fire in an instant. As Bolan started to get to his feet, another man charged through the doorway. Bolan swung his weapon toward the threat.

The attacker slammed the butt-stock of his T-68 rifle into the frame of the BA-52. The blow struck the weapon from Bolan's grasp. The warrior reacted swiftly, throwing a hard left hook to his opponent's face and grabbing the barrel of the T-68 with his other hand. Bolan drove a knee to the soldier's groin and shoved the rifle to keep the man off balance.

Another figure appeared behind the first. The warrior pushed the dazed soldier into the second man, but the guy reached forward and grabbed the warrior's hair. All three men staggered toward the doorway. More hands gripped Bolan's shirt and yanked hard. The Executioner was pulled through the doorway, outside, with at least three soldiers to deal with.

He rammed an elbow into the man holding him from behind, but his original opponent slammed a fist under the Executioner's jaw. The uppercut rocked the Stony Man commando. He tried to throw a punch in response, but hands seized his arms. They guy who hit him cocked back a fist to repeat the action, but Bolan swung a snap kick to the man's abdomen. The boot sent the fellow staggering backward.

An explosion erupted inside the heroin processing center as the second kerosene container went up. The blast startled the soldiers who held Bolan. He trod on the instep of one opponent and managed to yank his arm free, then smashed a backfist to the guy's face. Another soldier hooked a kick to the warrior's belly, and the pain in his side flared to sheer white agony.

He glimpsed a fist an instant before knuckles crashed into his face. Soldiers twisted Bolan's arms to hold him as others pounded him with fists and kicks. The Executioner's head reeled with pain, and his body felt as if he had been caught in a stampede. He had no strength left to fight, and the barrage of blows drove him to the brink of unconsciousness.

Suddenly the beating stopped. The warrior sagged in the grip of the soldiers. He barely breathed, his nose and mouth clogged with blood. His vision was blurred and his ears rang.

"Belasko!" a voice shouted. "Belasko!"

Bolan blinked to try to clear his vision. He raised his head and saw Colonel Thaung standing in front of him. The officer's face was as hard as a diamond mask.

"You are going to pay dearly for this," the colonel gritted. "I am going to put you through absolute hell. You will know the suffering of the damned."

Thaung lashed a booted foot between Bolan's legs, and the warrior's crotch exploded in agony. The pain became too great and he passed out.

19

Thunder disturbed Bolan's unnatural slumber. The sound pounded at his ears as consciousness slowly crept back, and with it came pain. His body ached and his limbs felt stiff and immobile. Thoughts and images tumbled inside his head. The confusion cleared and he recalled what had happened. He slowly opened his eyes.

His vision was blurred. The sound continued and he realized it wasn't thunder. Someone was striking something repeatedly with a hammer or a mallet. Bolan stared at the shapes until the mists drifted from his eyes. He saw his own arms extended before him. An H-shaped frame of bamboo had been erected, and his wrists were tied to the center bar and support poles.

The Executioner glanced over his shoulder and saw a large man hammering a stake into the ground. He recognized the person as the stick fighter who had killed one of his comrades in the *banshay* demonstration. The brute smiled at Bolan as he completed his chore. The warrior realized the stake had been driven to pin down a pole across the backs of his knees. The pole was tied to a stake at each end to secure it in place and trap Bolan's legs.

Captain Lat limped toward Bolan. The officer leaned heavily on a crutch. His wounded leg was heavily bandaged, and a splint had been set around the knee and lower thigh. He glared at the prisoner.

"I see you are awake. I believe you have an expression in English that suggests a person's mother was unmarried."

Lat suddenly slammed a fist into the side of Bolan's head. The knuckles jarred his skull, and Bolan nearly lost consciousness again. The captain raised his fist and prepared to strike again. Colonel Thaung appeared and snapped something in Burmese. Lat reluctantly lowered his fist. Thaung stepped closer. He carried a bamboo pole almost a yard long. The colonel poked the tapered end under the Executioner's chin and forced his head up.

"I told the captain to stop," he explained. "I don't want you knocked unconscious again. You should be wide-awake to appreciate what is going to happen to you, Belasko."

Bolan was aware that a crowd had formed around him. The whole camp wanted to watch. He realized that whatever Thaung had in mind, it was going to be the most cruel spectacle these hardened men had ever witnessed, and they were looking forward to the entertainment.

"You killed seventeen of my men," Thaung said, "including Maung Gawbyan. Several others are badly injured. You also destroyed a fortune in heroin and morphine. Months of labor for the men here were ruined. Our profits will suffer drastically for this, and we won't be able to meet the requirements for drugs to any of our contacts except some very small local dealers.''

"I didn't kill Gawbyan," Bolan said. "I think you're a lousy shot, Colonel. You missed me and nailed him."

Thaung spit in Bolan's face. The saliva slid down the American's cheek. The colonel stared at this captive with raw hatred in his eyes.

"You keep your mouth shut until I tell you otherwise. You have caused me enormous loss, Belasko. Worse is the loss of face I have suffered because I trusted you. I even liked you. This embarrassment and betrayal enrages me as much as the financial loss and the deaths of my men."

Lieutenant Po and Sergeant Gyi joined the others to look down at the prisoner. The sergeant's expression seemed calm and inscrutable. Bolan couldn't recall seeing a different expression on the man's poker face.

"You have dishonored us," the lieutenant declared.

"What do you people know about honor?" Bolan asked. "You oppress your own countrymen, you sell drugs that you know will destroy countless lives here and in other countries, and you use torture and murder to seek selfish ends. What evil code of honor condones that sort of conduct?"

"Nice little speech," Thaung jeered. "Now it is time for you to start answering some questions. No need to make any quick confessions. This is going to take the rest of the night and all of tomorrow. You seem to be in excellent physical condition. We may be able to drag this out for two or three days.''

Thaung stepped beside Bolan and raised the bamboo stave, lashing the Executioner's back. The first blow barely stung. The second struck the welt and caused some discomfort. The third felt twice as painful and the next blow made Bolan suck in a tense breath. The flogging continued. Bolan's back arched from the blows, but he was securely trapped and bound in place. There was nothing he could do except endure the torment.

''This is one of my favorite ways to begin interrogation,'' Thaung said. ''This can go on for hours. Eventually your skin will split open and the muscles will be pulverized. Nerve endings are raw and the pain is incredible. But, if it goes much further the nerves may actually go numb. That is when we move to another part of your anatomy. We'll get to every part of your body before we're finished, Belasko.''

Bolan realized Thaung was telling him this to increase fear. Torture was psychological as well as physical. He wanted the warrior to know that with every moment of pain he suffered, the next would be worse. The bamboo struck again and again. This was just the beginning. The flogging would seem gentle compared to the tortures Thaung planned for the prisoner.

The Executioner recalled his training. Most of what he had been taught concerned being a POW tortured by the enemy. The standard advice was to hold out for a while to convince the torturers you had broken and then tell them a convincing lie with enough truth to stand up under a general information check.

The old notions about never saying more than name, rank and service number had finally been recognized as idiotic, unrealistic and spiritually destructive. Any man would break eventually. It was absurd to consider a man a coward because he talked under torture. Sooner or later, he would either talk, die under the punishment or be turned into a drooling, brain-damaged imbecile.

A soldier didn't accomplish anything positive by getting himself killed in a POW camp. If he refused to talk, eventually torture would cause permanent injury or mutilation. A man in a weakened condition from starvation or beatings, a man who had lost the use of one or more limbs or any of his five senses was less likely to be able to escape or overpower his enemies if the opportunity was presented.

Great advice, and generally it would be the sort Bolan would follow. However, Thaung wasn't going to stop regardless of what he told him. The colonel continued the flogging for ten minutes before he even asked the first question.

"What is your real name?"

"Pan," Bolan replied. "Peter Pan. I was sent here in an effort to make me grow up."

The bamboo lash struck again and again for another five minutes.

"Your name?

"Leon Abrams. I'm a mercenary hired by the Triad because they're pissed off with you people."

"Liar!"

The lash struck again.

"Gawbyan was the liar!" Bolan said. "Didn't it ever occur to you that it was pretty weird how he got away when the other men at the restaurant were killed? How his men got killed later? All that dope and all that money just happened to disappear?"

"The only person who said the police didn't get the heroin was you, Belasko," Thaung replied. "Or Abrams. Whatever your name really is."

"I'm telling you the truth. Contact your fancy-ass Interpol chums in Hong Kong and see if they can't get a line on narcotics investigations in New York. Just see what really happened to that heroin!"

Thaung didn't strike again. He was listening. Bolan was buying time. What for, he wasn't quite sure, but it was all he could do.

"You're saying Gawbyan went into business for himself?"

"Damn right he did," Bolan said. "Son of a bitch recognized me. He knew I worked for the Triad. That's why he tried to finger me. Little bastard. I wish you hadn't killed him. Then he could be going through this shit and you could make him tell the truth."

"He's lying," Captain Lat shouted. "Gawbyan didn't betray you. This American pig is CIA or possibly DEA."

"Use your head, Colonel," Bolan said. "You think DEA or CIA or anybody else would send somebody Gawbyan knew?"

"What about the drug deal you claim you wanted?"

Bolan's story was putting him into a verbal corner. There were holes in it that didn't make sense, and he'd have to patch them with some sort of plausible explanation.

"You came to me claiming you represented Mafia interests that wanted a multimillion-dollar deal for four hundred kilos of heroin," Thaung reminded him. "Now, you claim to work for the Triad. I think the captain is correct. You are lying."

"The Triad suspected you might be doing business with the Mob already," Bolan replied. "They had me come as a fake Mafia buyer. They wanted to know if you'd go for the deal. See, they figure you're tied in with them and you shouldn't be doing business with anybody else. More important, they wanted to know if you had done any business with the Mob before. They got that idea from Gawbyan. Who the hell do you think he sold the dope to?"

Somebody spoke in Burmese. A short conversation in the language occurred. Bolan had no idea what they were talking about, but Thaung wasn't using the bamboo pole on him. Couldn't be all bad, the warrior reckoned.

"Why did you insist on seeing our heroin operation?" Thaung asked. "The Triad already knows about it."

"They figure they couldn't be sure of anything after what Gawbyan pulled," Bolan answered. "To be honest, I think they might plan to take control of this operation and hand it over to the Meo. Hell, you know the Chinese. They aren't going to tell a hell of a lot to a white man like me."

"More lies!" Lat spit. "Why did he start shooting? Why did he destroy the heroin?"

"I started shooting because those soldiers were about to kill me, you dumb shit! What would you have done?"

Lat raised his fist, but Thaung stopped him once more.

"How do you explain burning the heroin?" the colonel asked.

"I tossed the kerosene on it because I was going to threaten to burn the dope if you guys didn't back off and let me explain what was going on. Then your boys came charging through the door and a stray bullet ignited the kerosene. I'm not any happier about that than you are. Even if you people don't kill me, the Triad will. They really did want that four-hundred-kilo drug deal."

Lat was frustrated. "I don't believe a word of this, Colonel."

"I bet," Bolan said. "What the hell did you and Gawbyan have goin' together, Captain? How come you two became such buddies and didn't care if you jeopardized security here by coming in on a helicopter?"

"You lying bastard!"

"Gawbyan knew that tomorrow I'd be back in Rangoon and report to the Triad. They wouldn't be thrilled with Colonel Thaung, but they wouldn't be at all happy with Gawbyan. Probably not with you either, Lat. You really thought they wouldn't find out you and Gawbyan had your own deal going?"

Lat stood on his good leg and raised his crutch to strike Bolan. Thaung raised the bamboo stave to block the crutch. He uttered a curt order in Burmese.

"You probably are lying, Belasko," Thaung said. "You didn't tell us any of this until the beating began, and you made those snide, pious comments before about how disgusting we are because we are drug dealers, torturers and murderers."

The Executioner's mind worked rapid-fire.

"Hey, I don't like drug dealers or tyrants. I'm a mercenary. Before the political changes occurred and the wars in Angola and Mozambique were put on hold, I had work as an honest soldier of fortune. I didn't rape, pillage, torture or kill anybody who didn't deserve it. I think you people are scumbags. So's the Triad, for that matter. Maybe I gotta work for people like you, but I don't fuckin' like it."

Thaung seemed to be considering what he said. Bolan went for the next lie.

"The reason I didn't tell you right away is because I still wasn't thinking straight after you guys beat the hell out of me. I've been living this Mike Belasko cover to such a degree it was hard to let go of it. Look, I know this is hard to swallow all at once."

"It is making me gag," Lat said.

"Tough, pal. I'm talkin' to the colonel. You can get in touch with a Triad guy named Hal Kwoon. That's Jason Kwoon's older brother. Jason got killed in New York due to Gawbyan's treachery. Contact Hal Kwoon and he'll verify everything I told you."

"This is absurd, Colonel."

"Perhaps," Thaung replied. "I'm not certain what to believe at this point. Of course, you'll tell me the truth eventually. Pain has a way of dissolving lies."

"Sure," Bolan replied. "After a while I'll probably tell you whatever you want to hear if you'll stop the pain. That won't mean it's true. Haven't you forced confessions from people you knew damn good and well were innocent?"

"Why are we listening to this American spy?" Lat asked.

"You do seem to be in a hurry to silence him," Lieutenant Po remarked. "Why is that, Captain?"

Lat replied in Burmese. The junior officers exchanged angry remarks, but Thaung broke them off. The colonel was annoyed with both men. This sort of display in front of the troops was inexcusable.

"I'm going to radio Hong Kong," Thaung announced. "See if I can get any confirmation about some of these claims. If the Triad did hire this man, we should be able to find out through Interpol sources. They certainly have a file on Jason Kwoon and can easily find out if he has a brother named Hal."

"You're not going to let this bastard go unpunished?" Lat asked. "After everything he's done? I may lose this leg because of him."

"He still deserves to be tortured to death," Thaung said. "He caused too much damage to us, even if his reasons are true. You two work on him. Just bear in mind he needs to answer questions. He can't do that with a brain concussion, a broken jaw or if he goes into shock. Don't get carried away."

Thaung headed for the head shed. Lieutenant Po began flogging with the bamboo pole. He was less adept at this than Thaung. The stick struck at different angles and hit Bolan in a haphazard manner. The effect was far less painful than what the master torturer had done, but Bolan pretended every blow was agony.

Captain Lat looked down at Bolan with contempt and loathing as he took a pack of cigarettes from his pocket. He struck a match and lighted a cigarette. The officer puffed gently and limped in front of Bolan. He tapped off some ash and stabbed the burning tip of the cigarette into the back of the warrior's left hand. The Executioner hissed in pain as Lat ground the hot tobacco into flesh between his thumb and forefinger.

"You want to talk now, American?"

"I already talked, Lat," Bolan replied.

"We'll get you to tell the truth. You just need something more drastic to loosen your tongue."

The captain used another match to relight the end of his cigarette. He fixed the crutch firmly under his arm so he could use both hands. The officer seized Bolan's hair and yanked his head back. Lat blew on the glowing tip of the cigarette and pointed it at the Executioner's face. Bolan tried to pull away, but Lat held on to the American's hair as he moved the cigarette closer.

"You don't have to be able to see to talk," Lat said.

Bolan strained his neck to try to move his head as Lat lowered the cigarette toward his face. The evil gleaming tip hovered toward the warrior's left eye.

Lat chuckled. The end of the cigarette looked like a hot red coal encased in gray as it loomed closer to Bolan's eye. Smoke produced more moisture that seemed to cling to his lashes. The Executioner closed his eyes tightly, hoping the lids could hold up against the burning pain.

"Come now, Belasko or Aarons or whatever we're supposed to call you," Lat said. "Open your eyes and look. You ought to, because this is the last thing you will ever get a chance to see."

20

The gunshot erupted without warning. Bolan's head was yanked forward. Lat's grip on his hair had suddenly tightened and pulled forcibly. Voices cried out in two or three languages, none of which Bolan understood. More shots rang out, and Bolan heard the familiar metallic rattle of automatic weapons. Lat's grip relaxed and the fingers slipped from the warrior's head.

Bolan opened his eyes and stared down at his tormentor. The officer lay on the ground, a bullet hole the size of a silver dollar marring his forehead. His lifeless eyes stared up at the predawn sky. The cigarette was still clenched between his thumb and forefinger.

The Executioner glanced from side to side. Several troopers lay on the earth, uniforms stained with blood from the ragged holes in their bodies. Others bolted for cover or raised weapons to return fire. Bolan couldn't see where the attackers were positioned, but Thaung's forces seemed to have been taken completely off guard. Apparently none of the sentries were on duty because everyone had congregated to watch Bolan being tortured.

The roar of engines rose amid the snarl of automatic weapons. Two trucks advanced from the motor pool. The troops were confused, uncertain as to whether their people or the mysterious attack force drove the vehicles. One gunman raised his rifle to open fire on the trucks, but a sniper picked him off with a trio of rounds. Another soldier started to run, stopped in his tracks and turned to point his subgun at Bolan. The guy obviously decided if anybody ought to die, it should be the American.

The man prepared to trigger his weapon, but he was startled by the blaring noise of a truck horn. He turned and discovered the grille of the vehicle was only a few inches away and closing in fast. The soldier tried to jump clear. He didn't move fast enough and the truck smashed into him. The guy's shattered body was thrown four yards and fell to the ground in a mangled, crushed lump.

The truck came to a halt beside Bolan, the second rig stopping on the opposite side. The big vehicles formed protective walls around Bolan as gunfire continued throughout the base. The warrior remained bound to the bamboo poles, unable to move or turn his head enough to see who climbed from the cab of one of the trucks.

"We'll have you loose in a moment, Mike," a female voice said.

Bolan recognized the voice and strained his neck to try to see the woman. A slender figure, clad in jungle camouflage fatigues, knelt beside him. The lovely face of Yuzana was a welcomed sight. She cut the ropes at his wrists while someone else removed the pole from the backs of Bolan's knees.

"I don't know how you got here," the warrior said, "but you sure arrived at a good time. A couple more seconds and Lat would have used my eyeball for an ashtray."

Yuzana placed a hand gently to his bruised face. She seemed distressed by his condition. The Executioner tried to get up, but the circulation had been cut off to his arms and legs. Hands grabbed his upper arms and helped him to the side of the truck. He looked at the faces of the rebels who assisted him. One appeared to be about forty, but the other didn't look older than sixteen.

"You must rest," Yuzana urged. "The fight is ours now."

"I don't have any broken bones or a concussion, and I don't think I have any internal bleeding."

Bolan flexed his fingers and pressed his feet hard into the ground. Blood flowed into the limbs. He clenched his teeth as the numbness was replaced with a painful sensation similar to hundreds of pins being stuck into his flesh. The pain was a positive sign. Blood vessels and nerve endings were still working.

"That is more than a scratch," Yuzana said.

She pointed to the blood stains and charred fabric of his shirt at abdomen level. The powder burn still ached, and any movement caused pain. Metal shards were still embedded in his flesh, and he was bleeding.

"I've had worse. You're going to need every person you've got who can still walk and shoot a gun. Thaung has a small army here. A little smaller than it was before, but they probably still outnumber your people.''

The intensity of gunfire by the colonel's forces confirmed Bolan's observation. The troops had been taken by surprise by the rebel attack, but they had reached cover by the barracks and other buildings to return fire with furious force. The continuous clatter of mounted machine guns told Bolan that the soldiers had more than assault rifles and subguns in their arsenal.

''They're going to blow these trucks to hell,'' he said. ''A few grenades or a couple of rounds from a rocket launcher will do it.''

''Right,'' the older rebel agreed. ''Let's move!''

A salvo of machine-gun rounds ripped into the vehicle close to the enemy position. Glass shattered and the driver screamed as shards sliced into his head and face. Dust billowed from beneath the rig as stray bullets struck the ground by the tires. Bolan and the rebels ducked low and slipped under the second truck.

The Executioner spotted a Type-68 near the corpse of a soldier. A truck tire was planted on the dead man's chest, and Bolan couldn't reach the magazine pouches on the trooper's belt. He grabbed the rifle anyway. The rebels seemed to be armed with Chinese Kalashnikov look-alikes as well. He could get more ammo later.

They bolted for the questionable cover of the poppy fields where the majority of the rebel force was stationed. An explosion roared behind them. It was one of the trucks, taken out by enemy grenades. The second vehicle was destroyed two seconds later.

A few of the soldiers had fled into the poppies when the shooting occurred. They realized too late that they'd run right into the arms of their enemy. Bolan and the three rebels raced past the bodies of two soldiers, then stopped abruptly before they could reach the fields. Other troopers were engaged in a deadly version of hide-and-seek among the opium plants.

The soldiers attempted to use the crops for cover and concealment while trying to take out the rebels positioned there. They had the additional problem of trying to avoid being hit by the "friendly fire" of their own comrades. One trooper was struck between the shoulder blades by at least three machine gun rounds when Thaung's forces sprayed the area with a merciless volley of high-velocity death.

Another enemy gunner noticed Bolan and swung his assault rifle toward the warrior. Bolan instinctively aimed from the hip and triggered his borrowed T-68. The Executioner hadn't used a Chinese military piece for some time, but he was no stranger to the T-68 and similar weapons based on the designs of Mikhail Kalashnikov. Three 7.62 mm slugs split open the soldier's face, and the guy dropped from view among the poppies.

Byu Lone appeared at the far end of the field and waved at Bolan with a NATO L42A1 rifle, which was equipped with a sniper scope. Suddenly a large figure rose from a row of poppies near Lone. The stick-fighting killer attacked the rebel and swung his stave with fierce strength and accuracy. The hard wood struck Lone's rifle and sent it hurtling from the rebel's hands.

The Executioner tried to aim his rifle as he ran toward the combatants. He had seen the burly *banshay* expert kill, and knew the stave was as deadly as a gun in the man's hands. Bolan held his fire because Lone was too close to his opponent, and the Executioner could hit the wrong target while trying to aim on the run.

The killer lashed his stave at Lone's head. The agile freedom fighter ducked under the whirling stick and thrust a kick to the larger man's abdomen. The brute staggered from the blow, and Lone closed in before his opponent could use the stave. A punch to the side of the trooper's face kept him off balance. Lone unleashed another kick and booted the stave from the hulk's grasp.

Enraged, the big man swung a backfist at Lone, who weaved his head from the path of the malletlike fist and delivered another kick to the goon's battered abdomen. This time the trooper doubled up from the pain. Lone hit the guy on the point of the chin with a hard punch. The man started to totter unsteadily, like an oak about to fall.

Lone continued the *bando* assault. He charged forward and stamped a foot to his adversary's thigh and used it for a springboard. Lone hopped in front of the astonished soldier like a kangaroo and suddenly slammed his other boot into the side of the man's neck. Both combatants dropped to the ground. Lone was the only one to get up.

Bolan, Yuzana and the other pair of rebels jogged to Lone's position. The burning wreckage of the destroyed trucks effectively masked this position of the field from the enemy. Few machine-gun rounds threatened them at the moment, but the situation would change as soon as the disoriented troops regrouped to form a more rational strategy.

"You look terrible, Belasko," Lone said. "You shouldn't be running about in such condition."

"Where do you suggest I lie down and rest?"

"You have a point. And I have something for you."

Lone turned to reveal a small backpack between his shoulder blades. Bolan opened the flap, reached inside and withdrew a .44 Desert Eagle. A shoulder holster rig and two loaded magazines were also in the backpack.

"Thanks for remembering," Bolan said. "How many men—"

He glanced at Yuzana and corrected the statement.

"How many people have you got?"

"Twenty," Lone replied, "but I think we're down to fifteen now. The truck driver went up with the vehicle, and we lost three or four more when that machine gun opened up."

"We have to act quickly," Bolan told him. "Thaung's soldiers aren't professionals, and they weren't too impressive in actual combat. The colonel hasn't encouraged them to take action independently, but they follow orders like driver ants. If

Thaung can organize them and launch an intelligent counterattack, we'll have a major problem.''

Bolan strapped on the shoulder holster as he spoke. The welts from the bamboo flogging transmitted a fresh wave of pain as the warrior adjusted the straps. He clenched his teeth, accepting the discomfort as he jacked a round into the chamber of the big Desert Eagle.

''I am embarrassed to admit we planned this rather poorly,'' Lone said. ''When we saw the majority of the enemy forces gathered together in a group to witness your beating, I thought we'd be able to pick them off rather easily. Unfortunately, many of my marksmen seemed to pick the same targets and didn't do as much damage as I'd hoped.''

''Their forces have been whittled down a bit. I took out some of them last night. Added to the guys you wasted, I estimate we've got about thirty to thirty-five to deal with. How have you deployed your forces?''

''Most of us set up here. Half a dozen went to the west and covered from the motor pool until the trucks could move in to rescue you. Four more are covering the southeast. I don't know if any of them have been killed or wounded.''

Bullets suddenly chopped into poppies less than two yards from their position. The Executioner and the rebels dropped to the ground as the salvo of machine-gun rounds swept over them like metallic locusts. The enemy was aiming too high and swiveled the chopper from side to side like a lawn sprinkler. That would end as soon as someone with more combat savvy took over the gun.

"You have contact with the other positions?" Bolan asked, gesturing toward a radio on the rebel leader's belt.

Lone nodded.

"Weapons. What have you got besides assault rifles? Launchers? Grenades?"

Lone removed his pack and dug out two pieces of pipe, built in a manner similar to the old World War II "potato mashers." Crude by modern standards, but Bolan would take what he could get. He examined one of the grenades. It used a cap-cover pin at the wide end.

"What sort of explosives are in these things?" Bolan asked. "Black powder or a nitro compound with a buffer agent?"

"Nitro," Lone said. "Most of our grenades are black powder, but we brought our best arms for the occasion. The timers to fuses operate between two and five seconds."

"Five seconds?"

"I know. Quite a delay, but we make these weapons ourselves and some of it is a little unpredictable."

"Yeah," Bolan said. "Okay. The enemy isn't paying much attention to any positions other than this area. Contact your other people and tell them to advance in an extremely stealthy manner. They shouldn't jeopardize their security until they get the signal. Then they lob grenades at the barracks. The enemy must have had their heavy weapons stored in an arsenal there. That's our main concern and where the majority of the troops are located."

"What's the signal?"

"I'll toss the first grenade at that helicopter. That thing is the only way anybody can fly out of here. Pretty hard to track them down if they escape in the chopper. Even if they get to the vehicles in the motor pool, they won't get far in the jungle. If they use that dirt-path road, we can cut them off before they get a klick from here."

"You don't want the motor pool destroyed?"

"Not yet," Bolan replied. "We can use the fuel tanks to destroy the poppy fields by pumping gasoline through the irrigation system. Speaking of fields, tell the personnel among the poppies to stay low. Keep prone, and fire at the enemy to keep them busy. They should move from one position to another after each burst of gunfire or the enemy will locate them by the muzzle-flash of weapons and pick them off."

"You obviously have more experience in these things. We'll do it your way."

"One of us should go instead," Yuzana said. "Mike is injured...."

"I can manage," Bolan insisted. "I'm no good on the radio because I don't speak Burmese. To just hang back here and fire a rifle doesn't make much sense because I'm more familiar with the place than the rest of you. I've got a better idea where the arsenal might be because I was inside one of the billets. I didn't see where arms were stored, but that means at least I know where they aren't."

"There is no time to argue," Lone said. "Hand him two more grenades in case he needs them. Good luck, Belasko."

Bolan accepted the explosives. He left the T-68 because he already had his hands full. The Desert Eagle would take care of any opponent within a hundred yards, providing Bolan got a decent target. He took a deep breath and bolted from the field.

THE BURNING DEBRIS of the mangled trucks continued to generate billows of dense, dark smoke, which Bolan used to his advantage during his approach. The smoke screen would help to conceal him from the enemy as long as the wind didn't change abruptly. His wounded side protested the quick movement, and the warrior felt as if he had ice picks jammed into his skin.

Bullets sliced through the air near the warrior's position. He stayed low, trying to ignore the pain that coursed through his body. Bolan continued to use the fiery wreckage as cover and moved as close to the flames as the heat allowed. Sweat oozed from every pore. He stepped to the edge of the crushed machinery and saw the rotor blades of the helicopter on the parade field.

The Executioner yanked the cap from a grenade. He saw the pin jutting from the lid and knew he had activated the timer. He didn't trust makeshift explosives unless he had personally made them or a demolitions expert he trusted had done the job, such as Gadgets Schwarz of Able Team or Gary Manning of Phoenix Force. The warrior hurled the grenade and saw it land near the helicopter. Immediately he ducked.

Someone had seen him throw the grenade, and a volley of autorifle rounds hammered the wreckage near Bolan's position. He stayed down as seconds seemed to crawl by at a sluggish rate. The detonator had to have malfunctioned, Bolan thought. Suddenly the grenade exploded and proved him wrong.

The blast ignited the helicopter fuel tank and more burning debris tore across the parade field. Bolan stayed down as part of a rotor blade and other chunks of metal hurtled overhead. A series of explosions roared and the warrior glanced up. Pieces of both barracks blasted loose from the rooftops and walls. Lone's men were on the ball and had followed their cue as instructed.

The Executioner realized the enemy would be distracted and disoriented by the unexpected attack. He quickly moved along the smoking remains of the truck to get closer to the billets. Bolan recalled his brief visit to the interior of one of the buildings. There had been no arsenal located at the west end of the barracks, so the east end was the most likely location for one.

He hurled another grenade at the targeted billets. Once more, the timing mechanism seemed to take a frustratingly long time to detonate. A man emerged from the building and rushed to the grenade to try to throw it clear. Bolan drew the Desert Eagle and snapped off a single round. The big 240-grain Magnum slug threw the trooper against a wall. The body slumped limply to the plank walk a second before the grenade exploded.

The blast ripped out most of the wall, and part of the roof collapsed. Bolan saw the legs of a soldier pinned under the rubble. More grenades showered the barracks, and explosions destroyed the buildings, forcing troops to abandon the smashed remains. Two figures struggled with a machine gun. One man tried to hold the weapon and fire it from the hip while the other fumbled with the ammo belt.

The machine gun fired a wild, irregular spray in the general direction of the poppy fields. Bolan triggered the big .44 Magnum and took out the gunner with a shot through the heart. The other soldier gripped the ammo belt in both fists, paralyzed with fear. Rifle rounds from the rebels ended his terror forever.

Two soldiers spotted Bolan and opened fire. The Executioner drew back to the shelter of the charred vehicles and yanked the pin cap from his last grenade. He gripped the handle in one fist and the Desert Eagle in the other. The first two detonators had taken four or five seconds to go off, but Bolan couldn't be certain how long it would take for the timer to set off the fuse to the grenade in his fist.

A soldier bolted forward and swung a subgun in Bolan's direction. The Executioner's Eagle boomed, the recoil raising his arm overhead. His target slammed into the ground from the impact of the .44 Magnum punch. He quickly heaved the grenade over the remnants of the trucks, the explosion sounding a moment later. Bolan dashed to the edge of his cover and discovered several soldiers had been killed or wounded by the blast and the rifle fire from the rebel forces.

Although dazed and bloodied by shrapnel from the grenade, two troopers pointed weapons at the poppy fields as the rebels began to advance. The Executioner held the Desert Eagle in a firm, two-hand combat grip as he fixed the sights on the chest of the closer gunman and fired. The powerful projectile passed through the guy's torso and struck the second trooper in the left arm above the elbow.

Bone cracked and the soldier cried out in pain. He turned from the poppy fields, his broken arm limp and useless. The man saw Bolan and dropped the rifle he held in his right hand. The men of Thaung's goon patrol weren't real soldiers. Bolan knew a true soldier was motivated by a sense of duty and loyalty. This man was just a greedy opportunist in a uniform, a perversion of a soldier.

Yet, the man had thrown down his rifle, and Mack Bolan wasn't about to kill an unarmed man. His mercy only brought the trooper a couple of seconds of life because the rebel gunfire tore into the man's back and neck. Bolan saw the figure topple to the ground, blood flowing from half a dozen bullet wounds. He was glad he hadn't killed the man, but he wasn't sorry the trooper was dead. The Executioner had seen too many good men and women die to be concerned by the death of men in league with a conspiracy of murder, torture and drug trafficking.

Dawn broke as the battle reached it zenith. Sunlight displayed the smashed billets and numerous corpses strewed across the battlefield. Surviving members of Thaung's troops scrambled for cover, some racing for the heroin and morphine processing buildings. One of these structures had already been all but destroyed by the fire Bolan had used to burn the dope stored inside. The rebels pursued the soldiers, confident they had the upper hand.

Three troopers reached the head shed. One of them yanked the pin from a sphere-shaped grenade and prepared to throw it at Lone's freedom fighters. Bolan snap-aimed and triggered the Desert Eagle, the .44 Magnum missile striking the trooper high in the chest. The mighty round smashed bone and dislocated the man's shoulder. The grenade fell from the trembling fingers and landed on the plank walk. The wounded man dropped next to the metal egg, overpowered by shock and massive bleeding.

The other soldiers whirled to fire back at Bolan, unaware their fallen comrade had dropped a live grenade. The explosion abruptly informed them of this error, the blast punching gunmen to the ground forcibly and finishing off the wounded trooper.

Dazed, but still armed, the fallen soldiers started to rise. Bolan shot one of them through the sternum and sent the guy's body rolling across the dirt. Yuzana suddenly appeared and fired her T-68 rifle and drilled the second trooper with a burst of 7.62 mm slugs. The corpse flopped like a fish on dry land, then lay still, lifeless eyes gazing up at the morning sun.

The door to the head shed had also been blown open by the explosion. Byu Lone and another rebel jogged closer. Both had taken grenades from dead troops. More reliable than the rebels' makeshift ''potato mashers,'' the freedom fighters were clearly glad to have the enemies' grenades and an opportu-

nity to use the explosives on Thaung's base headquarters.

They hurled two metal spheres through the opening to the commander's quarters. The minibombs
exploded in unison and the shuttered windows burst.
Pieces of furniture, office equipment and a single
corpse spewed from the doorway. The rebels charged
the entrance with weapons ready. Lone fired a salvo
of T-68 rounds before he dived inside while another
man covered him. Yuzana jogged forward to join
them.

Bolan ejected the magazine from his Desert Eagle
and fed a fresh clip into the butt well. Rebel forces
had comandeered the light machine gun, and more
grenades from corpses, using them against the handful of troops clustered by the heroin processing center. The enemy was boxed in and didn't have a
chance.

The rumble of an engine was barely detectable
amid the gunfire and explosions. Bolan turned toward the motor pool and saw one of the Land Rovers suddenly bolt from the area and race into the rain
forest. He recognized the tall, lanky figure of Lieutenant Po in the rear of the vehicle as the junior officer adopted a stance with a BA-52 chopper in his
fists.

Two other men were in the rig. Bolan couldn't see
the driver or the other passenger clearly, but he suspected the man behind the wheel was Sergeant Gyi
and the third man might well be Colonel Thaung. The
Executioner ran to the motor pool and climbed into
another Rover. No keys were necessary. Bolan turned

the ignition switch and the engine growled in response.

"Belasko!" Lone shouted. "What are you doing?"

The warrior barely heard him and didn't bother to reply. He had some unfinished business to take care of. The Executioner wasn't one to leave a job with a major goal undone. He pushed the stick forward and the Land Rover charged after the fleeing vehicle.

21

The enemy vehicle plunged into the jungle, elephant grass parting beneath the onslaught. Ferns and the low-hanging leaves of banana trees weaved and sprang back as the Land Rover passed. The rig nearly disappeared, as if the rain forest were trying to swallow it up.

Bolan followed, the movement of the plants revealing the path taken by the other vehicle. Leaves slapped the windshield of the Rover and impaired his vision. The warrior realized he could smash into a tree, but he concentrated on the pursuit. The enemy was faced with the same problems, and he doubted they had ever previously driven into the jungle at high speed. They didn't have an advantage in the chase even if they had a passing familiarity with the area. Although they had been carrying out the operation at the base, Thaung and his chief henchmen had basically been working out of Rangoon for the past two or three years.

The Rover bounced over the rough ground and Bolan was nearly thrown forward into the windshield when he ran over a large rock that lifted the front end of the rig two feet off the ground. He clenched the steering wheel and kept on the trail of the fleeing vehicle. The rain forest wasn't suited for four-wheeling. Bolan knew they couldn't travel far in the dense foliage and unpredictable terrain. He just hoped the other Rover would be forced to come to a halt first.

A burst of submachine-gun fire suddenly tore at the leaves and branches of trees and ferns surrounding Bolan's rig. The enemy knew he was giving pursuit and one of them was trying to take him out. The shots were fired wildly. The enemy was having as much trouble finding the Executioner as he was having keeping track of them. A bullet struck the windshield and starred the thick glass. Bolan hunched his shoulders and stayed low.

He didn't return fire with the Desert Eagle. There was no sense in wasting ammunition trying to shoot an elusive and virtually invisible target. Apparently the enemy reached the same conclusion because the bursts of gunfire ceased.

Suddenly Bolan saw the rear of the enemy vehicle visible beneath a tangle of vines and branches. It wasn't much of a target, and it was more than a hundred yards away. The Executioner went for it anyway. If he could rattle their figurative cage, their flight could become even more rushed and reckless. Bolan drew the Desert Eagle and fired two rounds. He saw one bullet hole appear in the metal bumper of the enemy's vehicle before it vanished behind a veil of foliage.

The loud sound of metal connecting with something solid announced that Bolan's move had worked.

To some degree, at least. He didn't know if the other Land Rover had crashed into an object hard enough to wreck the machine or just tagged something in the forest. The warrior slowed his rig. He didn't want to charge into an ambush in case they decided to retaliate.

A ball-like object sailed over a tall line of ferns. Bolan needed only a glimpse to know the projectile was a grenade. He bailed out of the Land Rover and hit the ground feetfirst, knees bent to absorb impact. He dropped into a shoulder roll, his side seeming to catch fire again as his body connected with a tree trunk.

Instincts kept him moving despite the pain. The Executioner crawled around the tree trunk a moment before the grenade exploded. Shrapnel tore through leaves and grass near his position. He heard the groan of metal on metal and saw the Land Rover tip over from the force of the blast. It crashed to the ground and lay on one side, wheels spinning in the air.

Bolan inhaled deeply. The pain in his side was reduced as he relaxed his abdominal muscles. More blood oozed onto his shirt. The warrior forced away the pain and concentrated on his next course of action. He could go to the enemy or let them come to him.

The ringing of the explosion in his ears subsided, and he didn't hear an engine growl, or the thrashing of a large object in the bush. The enemy vehicle wasn't moving. They were on foot for sure. Maybe one or more of them had been injured when the Rover cracked up, but Bolan figured he had better assume he still had three opponents to deal with. He started to get to his feet when he heard a rustling among the bushes.

An expert in jungle combat, Bolan ducked low and used some ferns for cover. They were coming back to make sure he was dead. The Executioner gripped the Eagle in both hands and waited. He remained still, aware that movement and noise could be detected easily in a forest environment. The enemy chose to come to him, which meant they had to deal with those problems. All he had to do was stay put and stay alert.

He didn't have to wait long. The tall, lean figure of Lieutenant Po stepped out of the foliage, BA-52 in his hands. The officer spotted the Land Rover and pointed his weapon at the crippled rig. He frowned as he examined the wreck. He was obviously looking for Bolan and couldn't find him.

The Executioner still waited. Unless Po was the only survivor or the only one able to get out of the enemy rig, he probably wouldn't be alone. The sound of leaves and branches being shoved aside by a large moving object revealed that Bolan's decision to wait was a wise one.

A head and shoulders materialized among the bushes. Bolan recognized the stern features of Sergeant Gyi. The Burmese NCO's eyes widened with surprise when he suddenly saw the Executioner. Gyi started to point his T-68 rifle at Bolan, but the warrior was faster and blasted two .44 rounds into the sergeant's upper torso. Gyi went down hard, and Bolan was confident he wouldn't get up again.

Po's weapon chattered and bullets raked the tree trunk above the Executioner's kneeling form. He returned fire, snap-aiming at the blink of the enemy muzzle-flash. Bolan glimpsed Po ducking behind the Land Rover. The officer fired a short burst, chipping more bark from the tree trunk.

The warrior was running low on ammo. He had one spare magazine and the rounds left in the Eagle. Not an ideal situation for a sustained exchange. Bolan decided on a different tactic. He fired a round above Po's position to encourage the lieutenant to stay down. Then he quickly aimed at the exposed fuel tank and punched a .44-caliber hole in it. Another round followed and sparked against metal.

The gasoline ignited and the tank exploded. The vehicle blew apart from the blast, scattering debris across the jungle. Burning remnants littered the ground. An arm, viciously amputated at the shoulder, lay among the ruins. Bolan spotted another chunk of Po pinned under the dismantled hood of the Rover. The lieutenant was no longer a problem.

The Eagle was out of ammo and Bolan reached for the spare magazine to reload. Colonel Thaung suddenly stepped into the open, pistol in his hand. The DDSI officer smiled as he advanced, his gun trained on the warrior's chest.

"Drop the gun, Belasko," he ordered.

The Executioner wasn't a man who surrendered his weapon easily.

"I can shoot you in the gut, and when you go down, shoot you in both arms if you like."

Bolan dropped the Eagle and the magazine. He raised his empty hands to shoulder level.

"You have a way with words, Colonel."

"So do you. Not much time left for talk. However, before you die, I'd like to know why you did this. That mercenary story was an obvious lie, and I don't think you're DEA or CIA. The rebels didn't hire you, did they?"

"Believe it or not, I'm just a guy who didn't like what you were doing, Thaung."

The colonel stepped closer. He was less than two yards from Bolan. Maybe he was taunting the warrior to try to make a move, or maybe he was mentally rattled from having his entire operation shut down. Either way, Bolan needed a distraction.

"I suppose it really doesn't matter now," Thaung said.

"Not really," Bolan replied. "Of course, you have a rival in the regular army who planned this. He brought me into it along with the rebels. I volunteered. My own damn fault."

"Regular army? Another lie. You're trying to stall for time."

"Figure you can take that chance?"

"I don't think I can afford to let you live another minute."

A loud popping sound erupted from the fiery wreckage of the Land Rover. It resembled the reports of a small-caliber pistol. Bolan knew what it was. Po's corpse was still burning, and the flames had set off cartridges on the dead man's belt. Thaung's attention shifted toward the noise. So did the aim of his pistol.

Bolan would never get a better chance. He lunged and chopped the side of his hand across Thaung's wrist. The gun fell from the officer's grasp, but he responded swiftly and delivered a hard head butt to Bolan's face. Foreheads banged together and the warrior's nose felt as if it had exploded from the blow. He staggered back as Thaung swung a right cross.

The Executioner's left forearm blocked the attack, and he thrust his other fist into Thaung's abdomen, aimed at the solar plexus. He followed with a left hook to the colonel's jaw. Thaung's head danced from the punch, but he lashed out with a kick and slammed a boot into Bolan's wounded left side.

The warrior felt as if he had been gored by a bull, his body jackknifing from the kick. Thaung's other leg rose, and he whipped the boot to the side of Bolan's head. The second kick sent the Executioner to the ground. He landed on all fours, his skull ringing with pain and his side ablaze with agony.

Thaung closed in and kicked Bolan in the ribs. The boot struck his right side, almost a tap compared to the other blows. The warrior clenched his fists in the earth and turned suddenly, hurling the dirt into Thaung's face. The colonel pawed at his eyes with one hand and lashed out another kick. Bolan dodged the blind attack and got to his feet.

Barely able to see, Thaung threw another kick. Bolan blocked with a forearm to the guy's shin and jabbed a fist to Thaung's sternum. He tagged the colonel with another punch in the face. Thaung's head whirled from the blow, and his body followed as he spun and lashed out a backfist.

Bolan had seen him use this tactic back in Rangoon when he showed off his kick-boxing skill. He was ready for it. The warrior's forearm met Thaung's to stop the attack, and he hooked a karate kick in the colonel's kidney. Thaung groaned and Bolan hit him with another left to the jaw. A stream of crimson spewed from the Burmese officer's mouth. At least one tooth had to have come out that time.

Thaung was desperate. He swung a high roundhouse kick for Bolan's head, hoping to end the contest quickly. The Executioner ducked as the boot rose and Thaung's leg whirled into thin air. The momentum turned the colonel's body and he inadvertently presented his back to the warrior. It was a serious mistake, and Bolan quickly seized the opportunity to exploit it.

He chopped Thaung across the nape to stun him. Then he wrapped one arm around Thaung's throat and jammed his other forearm across the base of the man's skull. Bolan gripped the elbow of one arm and planted a hand on the other biceps to lock the forearm vise. Before Thaung could attempt a counterattack, Bolan stomped the back of his knee.

The colonel's body abruptly dropped, his weight plunging while his head and neck remained trapped. Vertebrae crunched as the same principle used for a gallows snapped the officer's neck. Thaung's body went limp. Bolan held the grip for a couple of seconds to be certain his opponent was dead. Satisfied, the Executioner left the corpse and gathered up the Desert Eagle. He ejected the spent magazine and shoved in the fresh clip. Then he headed back to the base.

THERE WAS NO DOUBT who won and who lost. The rebels suffered a few casualties, but every member of Thaung's conspiracy was dead. If any of them had surrendered, the rebels had decided not to take prisoners.

The fuel tanks from the motor pool were plugged into the irrigation system, as Bolan had suggested earlier. Some pipe was needed to make the connection, but the plan worked. The poppy fields were soon soaked with gasoline. The pipe was moved to disconnect the fuel tanks from the irrigation system before torches were hurled into the poppies. The fields burst into flames. The opium crop could have been the funeral pyre for Colonel Thaung's twisted dreams.

Bolan watched as he lay on his back. Yuzana and a rebel medic tended his wounds. The Executioner was impressed by the skill of the medic. Yuzana explained that the guy was a real doctor who had once had a good practice in Mandalay with the largest clinic in the city. His pro-democracy politics cost him his job, his home and a year in Insein Prison.

"They tortured him until he signed a statement denouncing the democracy movement and swearing allegiance to the present government," Yuzana said. "When they let him go he joined us at Camp 101. Many of our people used to be lawyers, doctors, schoolteachers and others who once had respected and well-paid professions. They lost everything because they dared to dream of freedom.''

The doctor removed the metal shards and treated the powder burns and the welts on Bolan's back. He applied disinfectant and gave Bolan a shot of penicillin. The wounds were not life-threatening, and the biggest hazard was the possibility of infection. They wrapped the warrior's waist with a bandage as Byu Lone approached, assault rifle canted across a shoulder.

"How do you feel, Belasko?"

"Like I've been shot at, beat up and whipped with a bamboo pole," Bolan said. "Other than that, I feel fine. They're patching me up pretty well."

"Sorry we didn't arrive sooner," Lone said. "We didn't know you would be traveling from Yangon by train."

"Neither did I," Bolan replied. "I didn't think you'd be able to find me out here."

"We knew where the railroad cut through Shan, but we didn't know where you got off the train. Took us most of the day to find out you departed into the jungle near Mawkmai. One of our associates works at the lumberyard there."

"One of the guys with the elephants?"

"You noticed?" Lone asked. "Luckily he recognized Thaung and remembered you. Not many whites get out to Shan State. When we knew the right direction, we just had to follow the tracks left by the trucks and Land Rovers. Of course, when we got closer and we heard shooting from your fight last night. That helped guide us, and when we were about five kilometers away we easily found the place. Electrical lights everywhere and a building on fire. Not too hard to find it under those circumstances."

"The military won't have much trouble finding this place either," Bolan said. "We'd better be moving, Lone."

"Yes. Fortunately the rain forest is green and damp enough to prevent the fires from spreading throughout the jungle. Not so lucky is the fact planes will be able to spot the fires pretty easily when the military decides to check on Thaung and his people."

"It's a long way to Rangoon."

"But not far to the Salween River," Lone said. "We can reach it in four or five hours. We go downriver and we'll be at the Thailand border by tomorrow evening. Better you don't return to Yangon. Someone might recall seeing you with Thaung. They'll be asking a lot of questions after this."

"Not many," Bolan said. "It won't be hard to figure out what Thaung was up to when they investigate this base. The authorities will know Thaung was involved in the heroin trade. Good chance they might figure Triads with the Meo in the state knocked him off for muscling into their business."

"That's fine with me. I'd just as soon the government didn't suspect the pro-democracy forces were involved in this. It wouldn't be good for our movement to be associated with the death of a DDSI field-grade officer, regardless of what kind of criminal activities he was mixed up with."

"They won't hear it from me," Bolan promised.

The march through the rain forest was easier than Bolan expected. The rebels took point and chopped through the bush with machetes. The warrior was encouraged to take it easy, and he was too tired to argue. The didn't carry anything except the Magnum and a T-68. The others hauled the heavier burdens of food and other supplies. They were all impressed with the Executioner and treated him like an honored guest.

They didn't have much food, but they insisted Bolan eat more than twice what each of them consumed. He realized it would be impolite to refuse their generosity. He had learned long ago that when help was offered it was best to accept it if it didn't put others in jeopardy. The rebels were showing their hospitality the best they could, and he didn't intend to belittle this.

Lone's people were adept at travel by river and canal. They set to work when they reached the Salween and hacked down ample bamboo for a raft. Bolan was impressed by their speed and craftsmanship as they bound the bamboo and tapped the hollow ends with mud. By dusk they were on the river and headed southeast.

The raft trip was pleasant compared to his recent ordeal. Bolan took advantage of the situation to sleep. He was in the company of trustworthy allies who were familiar with dangers in the area. It was safe to close his eyes and relax. The warrior slept more soundly than he had since he arrived in Myanmar. The rest was the best medicine he could hope for.

The pain from his injuries was reduced dramatically during the river cruise.

At daybreak they hid weapons in burlap bags and urged Bolan to wear a conical reed-woven hat. He remained seated on the raft when they passed through populated areas where fishermen and boat transport were plentiful. Bolan was much taller than an average Burmese, and he didn't want to do anything to draw attention to their raft.

Soldiers were stationed by some of the fishing villages. They didn't seem to have any interest in the passing boats and rafts on the river. There was obviously no effort to form a dragnet to stop anyone suspected of taking out Thaung and his base. It was possible the DDSI and SLORC wouldn't even try to find out who had killed the colonel and destroyed his opium scheme. More likely, the government would try to cover up the whole affair because it would be a major embarrassment to admit a high-ranking officer in the largest security department in Myanmar was running a heroin processing operation and smuggling drugs to the United States.

They had to walk to the Thai border. Lone accompanied Bolan, but the others remained in Myanmar. Yuzana only held his hand and squeezed it gently as a farewell gesture. Bolan saw sadness in her eyes. He nodded. The parting was necessary. His campaign in Myanmar was over, but her war continued. The Executioner would have another mission.

A CIA case officer who called himself Malloy was waiting for them on the other side of the Thai border. He had the rest of Lone's payment for the rebels' role in this mission. Lone surprised Bolan with a short embrace. Asians seldom displayed such intimacy with foreigners.

"We will welcome you to join us as a brother in our family," Lone said. "It has been an honor to fight alongside you."

"The honor was mine, Lone," Bolan assured him.

"When we achieve freedom in our country, I hope you will return. Use whatever name you like. We'll be delighted to have you visit us under more pleasant circumstances."

"Stranger things have happened. Good luck, Lone."

Malloy escorted Bolan to a car. The Company man took the wheel. He didn't seem to be much for conversation and probably resented having to do anything with the warrior. Malloy hardly looked away from the windshield as he drove the vehicle.

"Passport and wallet with a new identification are in the glove compartment," he said. "You'll also find money and an airplane ticket for a flight from Bangkok to Washington, D.C. We'll stop at a town nearby. I suggest you get a shower and some fresh clothes. You look like hell, and you don't smell all that great, fella."

"I don't feel all that great, either," the warrior replied dryly.

Bolan was glad to be going home. The mission had been bloody and difficult. Good people had died as well as bad in the battle at the enemy base. Yet, what good had he really accomplished? Had he even put a dent in the drug trade? Heroin and cocaine would continue to enter the United States and other countries a hundred different ways. Even if it could be stopped, there would still be crystal methamphetamine and so-called designer drugs whipped up in homemade labs for the dealers to sell to their customers.

Was it worth it?

The Executioner knew it was. He hadn't expected to win a war when he took on the mission. This particular battle was over, and he'd no doubt engage in another. The best any soldier could hope for was simply to do his duty and get the job done.

The hunters become the hunted as Omega Force clashes
with a former Iraqi military officer in the next episode of

by PATRICK F. ROGERS

In Book 3: **TARGET ZONE**, Omega Force blazes a trail deep
into the heart of Sudan. Trapped and surrounded by hostile forces, they must break out at any cost to launch a
search-locate-annihilate mission.

With capabilities unmatched by any other paramilitary
organization in the world, Omega Force is a special ready-
reaction antiterrorist strike force composed of the best
commandos and equipment the military has to offer.

Take
4 explosive books
plus a
mystery bonus

Mail to: Gold Eagle Reader Service
3010 Walden Ave.,
P.O. Box 1394
Buffalo, NY 14240-1394

YEAH! Rush me 4 FREE Gold Eagle novels and my FREE mystery gift. Then send me
4 brand-new novels every other month as they come off the presses. Bill me at the low
price of just $13.80* for each shipment—a saving of over 10% off the cover prices for all
four books! There is NO extra charge for postage and handling! There is no minimum
number of books I must buy. I can always cancel at any time simply by returning a
shipment at your cost or by returning any shipping statement marked "cancel." Even if I
never buy another book from Gold Eagle, the 4 free books and surprise gift are mine to
keep forever.   164 BPM AEQ6

Name   (PLEASE PRINT)

Address   Apt. No.

City   State   Zip

Signature (if under 18, parent or guardian must sign)

*Terms and prices subject to change without notice. Sales tax applicable in NY. This offer
is limited to one order per household and not valid to present subscribers. Offer not
available in Canada.

1991 GOLD EAGLE   AC-92R

In the aftermath of a
brutal apocalypse,
a perilous quest for survival.

by **JAMES AXLER**

The popular author of DEATHLANDS® brings you an action-
packed new post-apocalyptic survival series. Earth is laid to
waste by a devastating blight that destroys the world's food
supply. Returning from a deep-space mission, the crew of the
Aquila crash-land In the Nevada desert to find that the world
they knew no longer exists. Now they must set out on an
odyssey to find surviving family members and the key to future
survival.

In this ravaged new world, no one knows who is friend or
foe... and their quest will test the limits of endurance and the
will to live.

Step into the future with the second installment of

JAKE STRAIT

BOGEYMAN

by FRANK RICH

In Book 2: **THE DEVIL KNOCKS,** Jake Strait is the chosen hero of the hour as he tries to take control of an impregnable fortress called Denver.

Jake Strait is a licensed enforcer in a future world gone mad—a world where suburbs are guarded and farmlands are garrisoned around a city of evil.